**Readies - Text copyright © Emmy Ellis 2024
Cover Art by Emmy Ellis @ studioenp.com © 2024**

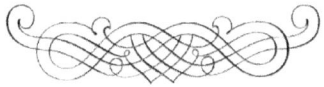

All Rights Reserved

Readies is a work of fiction. All characters, places, and events are from the author's imagination. Any resemblance to persons, living or dead, events or places is purely coincidental.

The author respectfully recognises the use of any and all trademarks.

With the exception of quotes used in reviews, this book may not be reproduced or used in whole or in part by any means existing without written permission from the author.

Warning: The unauthorised reproduction or distribution of this copyrighted work is illegal. No part of this book may be scanned, uploaded, or distributed via the Internet or any other means, electronic or print, without the author's written permission.

READIES

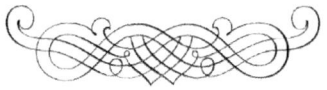

Emmy Ellis

Chapter One

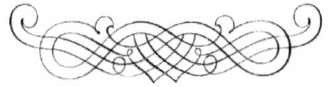

The police standing in the middle of living room confused Anaisha. What were they doing here? Mum and Dad never put a foot wrong, and her brother, Dayton, certainly didn't. Neither did Anaisha. Unfortunately, they all knew what the colour of their skin could mean, especially when it came to

coppers, so had Dayton been stopped on the street, accused of something he hadn't done?

Breathing while black. Existing while black.

Until she'd met Dad, Mum hadn't been exposed to all the shit that went on. Like she'd said, she'd lived in a bubble of privileged ignorance, viewing the world through a white lens. It had come as a massive eye-opener to see Dad victimised in various ways, her hounded for not 'sticking to her own kind', and she'd spent her life since then trying to protect him and her children from any racist bullshit.

It had become her mission.

"Mum? What...?"

Anaisha had come down from her bedroom at Mum's request. Mum's voice had held a warning, the one she gave when she sensed a bad situation coming up, and her tone was reedy, faint with a tinge of...what, panic? Now, everyone stood staring at each other, as if the two officers in uniform, one a man, the other a woman, both white, didn't know what to say or how to say it. Time had seemed to suffocate itself, just like the air wanted to suffocate Anaisha. It prickled with expectation, them waiting for the shoe to drop.

Dad would take a step back here. He wouldn't risk being told he was too belligerent, too loud, too black if he asked what was going on. Sadly, situations were manipulated into something they weren't so people got arrested for that. There was no doubt in Anaisha's mind that the police force was corrupt. Inherently racist. Not all the officers, granted, but even one was too many.

Mum got the ball rolling, as she always did when she needed to be the spokesperson so no one else in the family got into trouble or ignored. A lot of the time, people didn't respond to Dad, preferring to wait for Mum to answer any queries.

Even in this day and age. Would Anaisha ever live in a world where that behaviour no longer existed? She doubted it.

Mum stiffened her spine. "What's the problem?"

The man clasped his hands together. "Would you all mind taking a seat?"

"Not until you tell us what you're here for." Mum folded her arms, the warrior that she was, and positioned herself in front of Anaisha and Dad.

Anaisha stepped to the side so she could see her mother's expressions, read her, to know what might be coming next. Mum's racism radar was second to none.

She glared at the officers, tapping her foot.

"It's about your son," he said.

Mum rolled her eyes. "Here we go. Come on then. What's he being accused of doing? Because I'm telling you, he's a good boy, he isn't in a gang or committing crime like you might be thinking. I'm warning you, I'll fight this every step of the way if you've got him banged up for something on a trumped-up suspicion."

"It's nothing like that," the man said, "and I apologise if you've experienced anything resembling it in the past. Can we start again? I'm Quint, and my colleague is Raquel. Please, can we all sit down?"

Mum studied him for a moment, seemed to think he was one of the good ones, then turned and gave the nod to Dad and Anaisha. They sat in a row in the sofa. Quint and Raquel opted for the spare armchairs. Raquel looked as if she wanted to cry, and she toyed with a notebook, staring at the closed curtains.

Something bad must have happened. Anaisha felt sick.

Quint took the lead. "I'm sorry to have to inform you that your son was stabbed this evening. He passed away at the scene."

So blunt. So final.

Anaisha gasped in shock, Mum's vibrant scream tagging onto the end of it. Dad shot to his feet with an agonised wail—"Noooooo!"—that sent goosebumps up Anaisha's arms and tickling over her scalp. The room narrowed until all she could see was the doorway and the slice of hallway visible beyond.

Dayton. Stabbed. Passed away.

Her scream joined Mum's, and Anaisha kept screaming and screaming and screaming until her throat gave out and no sound emerged. She grabbed at the sides of her hair, pulling it, and someone drew her hands down, someone else banding their arms around her to pin hers to her sides. She shut her eyes, her mind going blank of everything except that her brother was dead.

She must have passed out, because she woke lying on the sofa, Mum sitting on the floor near her head, stroking it, Dad at the other end with her feet on his lap. For a second she didn't know what had happened, then it came crashing back, and she panicked, her chest constricting. The urge to run was so strong she had a struggle to remain where she was.

Quint and Raquel were still there, the latter actually crying, but two other people had arrived, both women, and they stood in front of the doorway.

The room was too full. Too everything.

How long had Anaisha been out?

"What…?" She sat up, her head going dizzy.

Mum got up and sat beside her, face stricken by grief; her laughter lines seemed deeper, and the hard set to her mouth hadn't been there before. Anaisha felt selfish for creating a scene. It meant Mum had swooped into mother mode and couldn't process the news like she should be because she was tending to Anaisha. Or maybe that was a good thing. If she had Anaisha to worry about, she wouldn't have to think, to accept, to feel the pain. Mum had always been the type to get busy when the chips were down. But what would she be like when the full force of what had happened hit her? Would she break?

"I'm sorry," Anaisha whispered. "Everything got...too much."

Mum put an arm around her. "Don't you dare say sorry. We all cope in different ways."

"Who are they?" Anaisha whispered.

"This is Janine, she's leading the case, and she's come to ask us some questions. The other lady is Grace, and she's a family liaison officer. She'll stay with us for a while, help us, all right?"

Anaisha nodded. "Why...how...?" She forced herself to ask the question: "Who stabbed him?"

At Janine's nod, Quint and Raquel vacated the chairs, said goodbye, and nipped out between Janine and Grace. The front door shut, and the women sat in the armchairs. A strange quiet settled over the room, a silence that seemed to breathe heavily. Anaisha shivered.

One of the newbies spoke. "I'm Janine. Take your time, and if you feel you need a break, just tell me, all right?"

Anaisha and her parents nodded.

"Tea," Mum said. "I forgot to offer you tea."

Janine smiled. "We don't need to worry about that, it isn't important, but if it makes you feel better, we'll have some in a bit. For now, I'd like to get as many facts as I can about Dayton, what type of person he was. I have to build a profile, and the more I have in our favour, the better it will be."

"He was the best," Anaisha said. "He was just the nicest person ever."

And he was. Always there for her, for anyone.

"He was a social worker," Mum said. "Trying his best to fix things one person at a time. He lived for his job, for making people happier. So who the hell wanted to kill him? Was it someone to do with work? Did they take exception to him stepping in and ensuring a client was safe? An angry husband or something?"

"He wouldn't hurt anyone," Dad said, the words broken. "He'd give you the shirt off his back, and I'm not just saying that."

Janine took this all in, her expression full of sadness.

*"Who **was** it?" Mum pressed.*

Janine didn't seem uncomfortable in the face of their grief, just compassionate, upset that such a good person had been taken too early. "The man who did it is called Shaq Yarsly. Do you know him?"

Anaisha gasped. Shaq was a little twat, strutting around their housing estate like he owned it. She couldn't stand the way he stared at her as if she were a piece of shit, and if she was with Dayton and they walked past him, he always sucked his teeth and called her brother names, her sometimes, too. It had been going on for years. Shaq was eighteen and had some balls on him — Dayton was ten years older, yet the kid didn't give a fuck who he hurled abuse at.

"Did Dayton work on a case involving Shaq? Could that be it?" Anaisha asked.

"We'll be looking into all avenues of Shaq's life to determine why he chose to end your brother's life. What can you tell me about him? Shaq, I mean."

Anaisha told Janine everything she could remember and how he'd made her and Dayton feel. "We thought he'd get bored, and it's been going on for so long that it became normal. He picked on Dayton more, saying he wasn't pure, you know, because Mum's white and Dad's black."

"That tallies with what he told me," Janine said. "A racial attack."

"But Shaq's black."

"It's still racial, love." Janine sighed. *"How did Dayton react to the taunts?"*

"He never chatted back, just ignored him. We both did."

"Sadly, he didn't ignore him this evening. Are you all okay for me to briefly explain what happened or would you rather not know? There won't be a trial, just sentencing, because he's admitted it, not to mention he was seen doing it by a couple of lads who held him until the police arrived, so he couldn't back out of it if he tried."

"Held him?" Mum asked. *"What, he didn't try to get away?"*

"No. Afterwards, he just stood there. That might seem strange, but some people commit crimes like that and then realise the enormity of what they've done. They're either in shock or they know they deserve to go to prison. People are complex."

"I want to hear all about it," Dad said. *"I want to know what my boy went through."*

Mum clutched Anaisha's hand. "What about you?"

Anaisha nodded. "I want to know."

Mum turned to Janine and Grace. "Okay…"

"The two lads were sitting at the bus stop when Dayton walked past. Shaq followed him, calling out

that Dayton wasn't a purebred, amongst other things. Dayton stopped and turned to him, asking to be left alone or he'd go to the police and report him for harassment. Shaq threw a punch. Dayton didn't retaliate, but he fell to the pavement and banged his head. The lads said it appeared he'd passed out, then Shaq bent over and used a knife."

"Just once?" Dad asked.

"No. Repeatedly."

Dad closed his eyes, a huffed sob parting his lips.

Mum squeezed Anaisha's hand to give them both strength. "How many times?"

"I'm not sure yet. There will be a post-mortem. My DS is with your son now. I asked him to remain at the scene in case other witnesses from the houses came forward—I like to be told new information immediately."

"He's still on the street?" Mum asked. "Oh God…"

"I'm afraid so, while we gather evidence and take photos, but he's beneath a tent."

"I want to go to him," Dad said.

Janine shook her head. "You can't, I'm sorry."

"Is Shaq sorry?" Anaisha whispered. That seemed the most important thing to know for some reason, and concentrating on that would block out the thought of

Dayton on the cold pavement, people in white suits all around him, his blood on the ground. How did they view him? As just a body? Or were they imagining who he'd been, the life he'd lived, and who'd been left behind to face this awful news?

Janine hesitated, then said, "Unfortunately, he hasn't shown any remorse as yet."

Right there and then, Anaisha vowed to make *him sorry.*

Even if it meant visiting the bastard in prison for the rest of his life.

Chapter Two

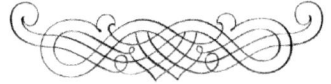

Months had passed since PC Anaisha Bolton had joined the Internet Crimes team on Operation Balustrade. She'd set up a username on London Teens, a place for kids to chat. As Loves_Risqué_Shots, she posed as a thirteen-year-old, hoping to catch the man who'd played a part in Summer Meeks' suicide. Summer's username, Mermaid, had attracted someone calling himself Fishy_For_Life, and she'd been persuaded to not only send intimate photos of herself but to leave money in coloured envelopes for him in locations of his choice. He'd bribed her. Said he'd tell her parents and friends about the pictures, plus plaster them on social media if she didn't put the cash in public rubbish bins. Once she'd left the last envelope, he'd vanished from the site, and she'd carried the burden of guilt and shame for revealing her body to him, thinking he was a lad around her own age.

Until it had become too much.

Since Summer's death, Anaisha had been chatting to someone calling themselves Amateur_Photographer. So far, he'd only asked for pictures of her face, but after studying other cases of this nature, she'd concluded that the grooming phase could take quite some time, so the more daring requests might not come for a while.

She sighed at the banal conversation on her screen. Was this even the bloke they were after? It was beginning to look like it wasn't, going by the type of thing this person liked to talk about, but she had to continue; it was her job now.

The team had access to Summer's laptop. They'd read all of the private, encrypted messages sent between her and Fishy via the London Teens site as her account was still open. Either Amateur wasn't who they were after or he'd changed tactics—Fishy had worked faster to obtain sensitive images from Summer, and so far, Amateur hadn't gone down that route.

Maybe he's being more careful since Summer's death hit the news.

Both people used the same VPN to access the site. Coincidence? What was disturbing was that they used a secret way to chat in the first place. The obvious reason was to hide their identity, they were up to no good, but what if Amateur wasn't a pervert and had only used it because he shared a computer with others and didn't want anyone knowing his business? Some teenagers were notoriously secretive, territorial over their privacy, and maybe this one had nosy parents and siblings who would take the mick if they found out he was talking to a potential girlfriend.

Hence why Anaisha couldn't help but think she was wasting her time here. It was halfway through the Easter holidays, so their communication time hadn't been hampered by

Anaisha and Amateur supposedly being at school. They'd spoken on and off all day Monday, so she'd gained a better perspective on who Amateur was portraying himself to be. Kind, considerate, obsessed with photography, and he didn't mind that she was of black and white ethnic heritage—he seemed to prefer it. He was respectful, the same as Fishy had been with Summer until he'd turned nasty on her, except Fishy had been more forthright in his bio, stating he preferred girls with no makeup and didn't like big breasts.

Who even writes shit like that?

Amateur listed normal things like going for walks with his dog. He'd responded in the correct way when Anaisha had told him she had photos of herself that would make his eyes pop out. He'd said she couldn't be too careful because the internet was full of pervs. But wasn't that something a groomer would say to put her at ease, to make her think he *wasn't* a pervert?

DCI Oliver Stains, her boss for this job, came over and sat beside her. He read the latest in the chat box, shaking his head. "He's either really clever, talking bollocks to you, biding his time before asking for other photos, or he's a genuine teenager—a really boring one. Maybe he's over sixteen, like seventeen or something, and that's why he's used a VPN. Doesn't want to get caught speaking to minors. If he takes it to the next level, he can get done for grooming and be put on the sex offender register."

"Hmm. I've said this before, but he could be being careful because the site was closed down while we investigated it. What if he thinks his words are being stored or read by the site employees? And while a sixteen-year-old lad going out with a thirteen-year-old isn't unheard of—kids do it all the time—when it comes to sex, it's a different matter. With the amount of information out there these days, teens know they can get into trouble."

Oliver let out a long breath. "What are your feelings on this? You're the one embroiled in a 'relationship' with him."

"It's a tough one, because we know grooming can take months, years even, so I keep waiting for something illegal to happen, but on the other hand, he's coming across as a kid."

"Or someone bloody good at pretending to be one. I mean, look at you, you're doing the same thing. He believes you're thirteen—or we assume he does—yet you're in your twenties."

"True. Maybe it's time for me to push for a meet. If he's cagey, we know something's off. Then again, he could be shy. Speaking on the internet is infinitely easier than doing it in person for some people." Anaisha included herself in that. While she was good at her job in uniform and being sociable came easily these days, at first she'd had to force herself out of her shell in order to deal with the public. "This lad—if it *is* a lad— might well be an introvert who becomes an extrovert in front of a keyboard."

"Keep going for a while longer. We can't risk letting this go in case he moves on to someone else, not to mention it'd be all our hard work down the drain."

"What I've been thinking about lately is, if this is a lad, then what I'm doing is wrong, right? He thinks he's talking to another kid."

"But we have the law on our side. You haven't said anything inappropriate, and we've gone into this on the suspicion that this is Fishy using another name. The picture he sent you of himself is available to buy on stock sites, so why, if he's sixteen, would he want to hide who he is?"

"Because he doesn't think he's attractive?"

"Once we see him in person, we'll have our answer. I agree with your proposal. Ask for a meet." Oliver gestured to the screen. "I see he's supposedly had to go and help his mother with the housework. Pop a message up now, then go for your lunch break."

Loves_Risqué_Shots: Hey, I've been thinking. How do you feel about meeting up? We could go to the cinema or something. No worries if you'd rather not. The other lad I asked didn't want to. Got to go for a bit — Mum's calling me.

Anaisha put her account on away and stood, stretching her muscles. "Back in an hour."

She left the open-plan office and went into the staff area, taking a sandwich and a bottle of water out of her locker. Needing some fresh air, she walked towards the front of the station.

Janine wandered down the corridor. She seemed lost in thought and looked tired. A slight baby bump bulged beneath her jumper. She caught Anaisha's eye and smiled. "Any news?"

"Sadly not. Well, only that we're now wondering if Amateur is a kid after all."

"Bugger." Janine glanced at Anaisha's sandwich. "Are you off out?"

"Yeah, I need to get away from here for a bit."

Janine checked her phone for the time. "I'll come with you if you want some company."

Anaisha nodded. She liked Janine and had spoken to her often after Dayton's death, even more so since the start of Operation Balustrade. Janine had been called out to the park where Summer's body had been found. She worked on the murder squad, so it had been her job to determine whether Summer had been killed. Once it had become clear it wasn't murder, after Summer's parents had received a delayed-send email suicide note from their daughter, Janine had been pulled off the case. It didn't stop her from asking about Balustrade, though, as she was invested in Anaisha's team catching the man who'd had a hand in the teenager taking her own life.

"Let me just get a cup of tea in my flask," Janine said. "No coffee for me anymore." She patted her tummy and walked off.

A few minutes later they left the station, heading in the direction of a small park round the corner.

"Now I'm pregnant, I have a whole new perspective," Janine said. "You know, how parents must feel when they lose their children. It's changed the way I deliver death knocks. I wish I'd been the one to call round your house regarding Dayton instead of uniforms, but on that occasion I was so incensed with Shaq, I opted to speak to him first."

Dayton being stabbed was the reason Anaisha had become a police officer. Janine had led the case, a godsend with how she'd kept the family up to date with information, and Grace Harper was a good friend of Anaisha's to this day.

Maybe I should speak to her about my problem…or bend Janine's ear?

Shaq Yarsly hadn't liked the fact Dayton had been of black and white ethnic heritage, saying he wasn't "pure" and was an "abomination". An utterly ridiculous viewpoint, but one he still stood by today in prison. Anaisha visited him, trying to understand him, waiting for an apology, but it was a waste of effort. Still, she couldn't seem to stop herself from going. Although he claimed to hate her, he always turned up for her visits.

It didn't make sense.

Maybe it's because I buy him cakes and a coffee from the café there.

She shook herself out of her head. Janine had been talking, and she hadn't heard a word.

"Err, are you okay?" Janine asked.

"Sorry, I was miles away, thinking about Dayton. What did you say?"

They sat on a bench, Janine sipping from a Thermos cup.

"I was going on about Shaq. The usual. What a bastard he is."

Anaisha opened her sandwiches. "Do you want one?"

"No, ta. So, how are you finding working with Oliver and that lot?"

"I prefer it. I don't have to worry about being assaulted. Then there's the verbal abuse—no more of that in an office." Anaisha took a bite of her sandwich.

"Hmm, I remember it well from when I was a PC. You still get it as a detective, but it happens less often. Is that what you plan to be?"

"I'd love it. Oliver said he's put in a request for me to stay on his team; we've just got to wait to see if it's approved. I could go for my DC exam early on the fast-track programme."

"Good for you. Do you know Bryan Flint at all?"

The switch in subject was odd and abrupt. "I've seen him around to nod hello to. Why?"

"He's someone you could get some pointers from. His career path went the same way as yours. Response copper, then he was brought onto a team to help out, and he's never looked back."

"I might see if he'd like a chat, then."

For a while, they stared at a young mother with her two toddlers by the swings. Mum had been like that once, having two kids. Her identity had been ripped apart with Dayton's death, and she'd struggled to work out who she was after that. For a while, having just one child hadn't seemed enough, but lately she'd been immersing herself in a project much like Dayton's work, where she helped others.

Anaisha finished her lunch and drank some water. Sipped. Again contemplated opening up to Janine about her recent troubles, the ones in her private life that had thrown her for a loop. But she had a feeling the DI would tell her to file a report, kick up a fuss. Anaisha wasn't sure she wanted to do that at the minute.

She switched her mind off of Ben, her boyfriend, and watched the daffodils at the edge of the park bobbing their heads in the breeze. Fluffy white clouds scudded along. It was warm enough to get away with no coat, and it was days like this when she wished she wasn't stuck at work.

But being at home isn't too nice at the minute.

"I heard all The Network people have been caught now," she said for want of something to say.

"It's a bloody relief, I can tell you. My boyfriend gave up work to be my bodyguard, you know."

"Blimey. It was that bad? You needing to be protected, I mean."

"It was."

"How come you never said?"

"I don't like to draw attention to myself. Cameron's gone back to his job now, but it's weird not seeing him in my rearview all the time. Still, I've got Colin, although I can't say I've got much confidence in him keeping me safe."

"Your DS is a bit weird if you don't mind me saying. Never seems quite with it."

"Hmm, he's a lazy sod who's living for his retirement date, although lately he seems to have decided to get more involved. I've got a feeling he's going to stay on and retire a lot later. I prefer him not sticking his hooter in, I'm more of a lone wolf in that respect. What about you?"

"I enjoy teamwork to be honest. One of the crowd. Being told what to do rather than taking my own initiative. Going out on response scared me sometimes when I had to make an immediate decision. I was never sure it was the right one, despite all the training, and there's always the worry of being knifed. What happened to Dayton will always affect me like that."

"You and I both know you learn on the job. Sounds like being a desk copper is more your thing, then."

"Hmm. I'd love to be secure enough in a relationship to be her." Anaisha nodded towards the mother and kids. Truth was, she *had* been secure with Ben once.

"I can't imagine being her. I never wanted children—long story short, I didn't want to become my mother—and I can't get my head around having to go to the park or those play centres. As for mother-and-baby groups…bloody hell, can you see me doing that?"

Anaisha laughed. "Err, no, but you never know, you might enjoy it."

"We'll see. I should go back. I didn't tell Colin I was nipping out, not that he'll even notice."

"I'll come with you."

They set off for the station.

"What are you working on at the moment?" Anaisha asked.

"A domestic murder. A woman killed her husband after years of abuse. Considering all the evidence we have to hand at the moment, I'm inclined to say it was self-defence, but time will tell. I need a few more chats with her to gauge whether she's telling the full truth or not. Grace is staying with her and the kids, seeing if she can pick anything up that points to the woman using abuse as a cover-up for just wanting to get rid of him."

Anaisha winced. Was that how *she'd* be seen? As making it up? Would whoever she confessed to believe Ben over her? "Must be hard because you automatically want to help when it's a DV situation."

"Yes, but in my line of work, what's on the surface isn't always the truth. She's saying all the right things, but I don't know... D'you know, I'm actually looking forward to having time off, away from all this madness, then when the baby comes, trying to be a decent mother. How's your mum by the way?"

"She's a lot better since she joined that group you told her about a while back. She's got a focus, helping other families who're going through the same thing, but it's still like she's in limbo a lot of the time when she's at home. Maybe doing what she does for the group makes her feel like she's carrying on Dayton's work in his place, and she has to put a brave front on for their sakes. Then when she gets home, she can be her real self."

"I'm glad it's helped a bit. You never know, it might seep into her homelife eventually. And your dad?"

"Still lost. He'll never be the same. He goes through the motions—gets up, goes to work, comes home, eats dinner—but he's a robot. He's like me, he just wants an apology, some form of remorse from Shaq about what he did."

"And you?"

"Trying my best to get Shaq to change his viewpoint."

"You're still visiting him, then."

"Every so often."

"I understand why you'd want to help him see the light, but he's a nasty piece of work, love, and I think you're wasting your time. By all means, if it's helping you through the grief, keep doing it, but make sure it doesn't become a crutch."

Janine put the keycode into the number pad beside the front door of the station. "Back to the grind."

They went inside, Anaisha returning to her desk. She hadn't had the whole of her break, but Amateur had replied in her absence regarding the proposed meet, so she couldn't resist diving back into work.

Amateur_Photographer: When?

She took a moment to compose herself, then called Oliver over.

"What's the best response?" she asked him.

Oliver stared at the screen. "Say tomorrow. It'll give us time to get people and a plan in place. Ask him to meet you in front of the Odeon, then say what you'll be wearing. Get him to tell you what he'll have on so we can watch for him."

"But what if he doesn't wear it?"

"Then we'll know he's not on the level and doesn't want to be seen."

Anaisha did a quick Google search to get her facts straight.

Loves_Risqué_Shots: Half one tomorrow afternoon, the Odeon on Bridgegate Street. *Ghostbusters* starts at two. I'll put on a red jacket so you know who I am.

Amateur_Photographer: I already know what you look like, you sent pics.

Loves_Risqué_Shots: Oh yeah. Duh. So what will you wear?

Amateur_Photographer: Err, you've seen my pic, too.

Anaisha stared up at Oliver. "What? I mean…he really thinks he can get away with that? He won't look anything like the stock site photo!"

"If he's a bloke and turns up thinking you'll be in a red jacket, and you can't see him, he could plan to approach you. Okay, that's not a problem, our team will be there to protect you, but if you weren't a copper and this was happening to a child… I don't like this at all. He's prepared to come out into the open and possibly risk you screaming or something if he asks you to go with him."

"I'd better answer him. Shall I call him out on his photo?"

"Yes, see what he says."

Loves_Risqué_Shots: I know, but there will be queues of people, and I'll see you faster if I know what I'm looking for. Plus I did a reverse image on Google, and your pic's from a stock site, so it isn't even you.

Amateur_Photographer: I take photos, remember. I upload them on there to make a bit of money. It's me, trust me. But okay, Man Utd shirt, so we're both in red.

Loves_Risqué_Shots: Wow, you never said you made money like that.

Amateur_Photographer: It's just a hobby at the moment. Got to go, Mum needs help with the shopping. Boring!!! See you tomorrow if we don't speak before then. [heart emoji]

"Shit," Oliver said. "Go on that stock site and have a look at the account associated with the photo."

Anaisha accessed it, going straight to the image which she'd saved in favourites. "Just a load of random numbers as his artist name." She clicked onto his portfolio of pictures available to download.

Oliver pointed. "He's definitely from London. Look at all the local landmark pictures."

"What if he's telling the truth and he's a kid? Then I've wasted all that time talking to a child while the real pervert is speaking to some other poor girl."

"But what if he's lying?"

Anaisha nodded. They'd soon know tomorrow. In the meantime, she'd comb through their conversations yet again, trying to spot a tell, anything that would say this was a man.

Sadly, she no longer believed it was. Then again, should she trust her instincts anymore? She'd thought Ben was a nice bloke, but she'd soon learned different. People only showed you the colours they wanted you to see, then when the time was right, they revealed the previously hidden darkness of their palettes.

She'd probably got this all wrong and Amateur was a paedo.

Chapter Three

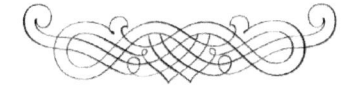

The refuge had been completed last month and now housed five women: four singles and one with two kids. More would arrive soon. George and Greg had employed an ex-social worker to manage it, a no-nonsense but kind-hearted woman called Sharon Turnbull who wasn't averse to being involved with The

Brothers. She was the type to want to get the job done by any means necessary and had confessed she'd bent the rules in her previous role. So long as she got people on the right road, she'd do whatever it took. She'd chosen her own staff, women she'd known from her old job, and the three of them lived in the place the twins had named Dolly's Haven. After all, their mother had been abused like the people it was designed for, and it seemed fitting, a lasting memory to remind them of the reasons why they were doing this.

George bloody loved the place.

High brick walls surrounded the large property, and key-coded, steel-lined wooden gates prevented anyone from just walking in. For the purpose of any frightened women who needed to be given entry quickly after they'd escaped their homes, a steel-lined door stood in the wall beside the gates, a bell push and keypad on the frame, a camera above. For outsiders, a rumour had been planted once the sale had gone through—a rich singer lived there alone, a recluse, and those who visited were his employees. A cook, a cleaner, that sort of thing.

Dolly's Haven, situated at the edge of a housing estate, stood four stories high and ten rooms wide, tall trees surrounding it, making it difficult for anyone to see through the windows if they stood on the pavement on the other side of the road. Voiles also helped. Other spacious homes completed the row. Small residential houses stood opposite and backed onto the street, lofty firs at the bottoms of their gardens, further securing the women's privacy.

Prior to opening the refuge, they'd chatted to Sharon about what those seeking help would need. Clothes, shoes, toiletries, towels, everything had been purchased in case people arrived with nothing. If such things as pushchairs were required, it would only take a quick trip to Argos, like they'd done for Calista's little one. With Sharon still in contact with people she used to work with, she'd been able to let former colleagues know about Dolly's Haven and that it could house twenty occupants. It was now on an approved list of places men and women could be referred to, and Sharon was down as owning it. Vic held therapy sessions there once a week, and a nurse was on hand to visit if necessary. The last employee they needed to find was a teacher.

George nodded to the security guard standing by the wall door and used their remote control to unlock the gates. They swung open quickly. If any enraged exes found out where their women had gone, security would send them packing. He nipped the BMW onto the grounds, a motion sensor picking up when his rear bumper had cleared the gap, the gates shutting swiftly behind them.

He drove round the back to the staff car park and cut the engine. "Ready?" he asked Greg, or maybe he was asking himself.

He'd found seeing and speaking to abused women who'd run away from home wasn't as satisfying as he'd imagined. He'd suggested opening the refuge so he could feel like he was doing something in their mother's memory, and for Ineke, Greg's Dutch girlfriend, but when he'd first heard this lot's stories, he'd had a hard time keeping the tears back. Their abusers would be dealt with in due course by Diddy and Kaiser, brothers who'd been employed to round them up when the time was right. The twins had helped their sister recently, and Stacey now ran one of their hairdressing salons, Curls and Tongs. She'd be here tomorrow to give the ladies a cut and blow-dry.

Greg unclipped his seat belt. "Yeah, as ready as I'll ever be."

They got out, going to the boot to collect the bunches of flowers and boxes of chocolates, plus the bags of toys for the kids. Tasha, aged seven, and baby Archie had already been given their teddy bears, ones every child would receive as a comfort after they'd been wrenched out of the only homes they'd known, and there were other toys in the playroom, but George had a soft spot for the nippers, and several items had just happened to make their way into his online basket.

Sharon would have been alerted to their arrival by a buzzer inside linked to a motion detector, and she stood at the front door, Archie asleep in her arms. She'd taken to the baby and helped Calista out a lot by minding him for her. "I'll just pop him down in his cot."

She walked upstairs, and the twins went inside. Tasha's laughter floated out from the playroom, such a good sound to hear, considering she'd been withdrawn when she'd first arrived, bursting into tears at the drop of a hat.

George poked his head around the door. "Who can I hear giggling?"

"Uncle George!" Tasha jumped up from doing a puzzle at the table with her mother, launching herself at him, her cheek squashed against his belly. She stepped back and eyed the bags. "What's in there?"

"Well, someone told me you've been a really good girl, being brave for Mummy and Archie while you settle in, so I reckon you should have a present or two."

She glanced at her mum. Calista's eyes welled up.

"Can I have it?" Tasha asked.

"Of course you can." Calista dabbed at a tear. "I can't thank you enough, George."

"Like I've said before, you can thank yourself for having the courage to get away."

He walked over to the table and took out a gift-wrapped box he knew damn well Tasha would want to see first. She was right up his arse, excited, and he handed it to her. She ripped open the pink paper and stared at the contents.

"Fucking hell, look what he got me!" She looked over at her mum again. "Sorry…"

"I'll pretend you didn't swear this time," Calista said, "but remember what we said. No matter that Daddy said it's okay for you to do it, it isn't nice, and you mustn't say that sort of thing until you're an adult, all right?"

"All right." Tasha stroked the box, smiling at the Barbie staring back at her. "Did Archie get anything?"

"He did, and there's another one for you." George removed it from the bag.

Tasha didn't seem to want to let the Barbie box go.

"Do you want Mummy you open it for you?" George asked.

Sometimes, the little girl needed prompting, a nudge in the right direction. She'd lived a strict life while her father was around, her mum trying to make up for it when he wasn't by joining her in playing with her old Barbies, which she'd had to leave behind when they'd fled.

Tasha nodded, and Calista peeled the paper off, revealing a Barbie car. Tasha burst into tears, clearly overwhelmed, and a lump hurt George's throat. He couldn't wait to beat the shite out of her father—or worse—but Calista hadn't decided yet what she wanted to happen to Morgan Nivens, tosser extraordinaire.

Each woman had been warned—but in a gentle way so as not to frighten them any more than they had been in their violent relationships—that this location and anything that was discussed here had to remain confidential, and that death, should it occur, would never be mentioned outside these walls. After they'd stayed here for a while and were deemed safe enough to venture back out into the world, they'd be offered a place to live. Last month, George and Greg had bought a block of forty flats. A furniture project place had agreed to do a charity drive to encourage the residents of Cardigan to donate items of furniture, and the whole thing had a community spirit vibe to it.

Mum would have been tickled pink.

George cleared his throat. "I'll just see how Greg's getting on."

He popped Archie's bag of gifts on the floor and left the room, eyes itching, and found his brother in the large communal kitchen. Four tables that seated six apiece stood in the dining side, and the other women sat around one of them, each with a bunch of flowers and a box of chocolates in front of them. All had been crying, their eyes red, but they now laughed at something Greg had said prior to George's entrance.

"Everyone having a good day?" He sat at the next table along.

Nods and chatter filled the room, and he turned to the cook, Lucia, who used to work in a school kitchen. She buttered bread, and an array of fillings in Tupperware boxes sat in a row at the back of the worktop. She was sixty-two, a widow, and had come out of early retirement to live here. She'd apparently found her tribe, so she'd said, and her compassion stood out a mile.

George basked in the emotions rolling through him. They were doing good here instead of the bad they were known for, and each woman appeared a damn sight better than when they'd first arrived. Rosy cheeks, that hollow, haggard look gone. Lots of smiles, shoulders no longer up by their ears. And hope, it shone from them, their futures bright instead of bleak. They had a purpose now Vic had taught them the abuse wasn't their fault, they didn't deserve it. All of them had enrolled in online courses to learn a new trade, and the twins would offer them jobs later down the line.

Calista wandered in. "That's Tasha sorted for a while. The toys are out of the box, and she's driving Barbie into town to get some new clothes, apparently." She sat at George's table and glanced over at the door.

Sharon came in and walked to the sideboard, switching a video baby monitor on. "Archie woke up when I put him down, but he's settled again now. Anyone fancy a game of cards?"

Women got up and pushed tables together. It had a family feel to it, them knowing what to do in sync, and seeing as they'd all been living together for a couple of months now, it made sense. Lucia brought over a pile of sandwiches, putting the serving plate in the middle of the two tables. Greg went to the fridge and carried cans of Coke over, and Sharon took a pack of cards from the sideboard drawer. The cleaner, Hattie, appeared, carrying laundry bags full of sheets and towels washed and pressed at Lil's Laundrette. She did the clothes here, the utility room containing two washers and dryers and an ironing station. She nodded at them all as a greeting and nipped through to the storage room.

Pride filled George. Their vision had created this—*his* vision—and he had to admit crime *did* pay. All right, Dolly's Haven and the flats had been bought using legitimate money amassed from Jackpot Palace, their casino, but if they weren't bully boys and didn't run Cardigan, this place wouldn't exist. These women wouldn't be happy, and some of them would even be dead.

The thought of that angered him.

He got up to make himself a coffee using the fancy machine he'd insisted on buying. He stood there and drank it, watching the fun, Greg getting stuck in, claiming he was going to beat them all at gin rummy. Tasha popped into the hallway on her knees, pushing Barbie around in her car, eventually coming into the kitchen. George reckoned she couldn't stand being away from her mother for too long. Maybe she had the sense she had to protect her still, which was something she'd tried to do at home. She was homeschooled now, online, but that would change when a teacher arrived. The fact she'd had to be ripped out of her school and away from her friends because of her father boiled George's piss. They couldn't risk him turning up there and snatching her, even though Calista had taken him off the approved pickup list.

Nivens wouldn't know what had hit him once Diddy and Kaiser got hold of him, or maybe George and Greg should pull the bloke in. Stacey's brothers had proved they loved beating pests up, and George regularly sent them out to *persuade* people to pay protection money or behave on the Estate. They'd become valued members of the Cardigan team.

Tasha spotted the sandwiches on the table and, standing, she tucked Barbie and her car under her arm so she could collect a plate and some food. She eyed the stack of Cokes, looked at Calista, and smiled at the nod she received.

"Just this once," Calista said.

Tasha settled at one of the other tables, parking Barbie in front of her plate. Fuck, how many other kids were in need of this place? How many were right now being shouted at or scared to death by an abusive parent?

Too many, and while George conceded he couldn't save them all, he'd give it a bloody good try.

Chapter Four

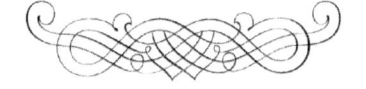

Terry Meeks would never get over the loss of his daughter, nor would he give up trying to find the scumbag who'd pushed her into killing herself. Many a time he'd thought of picking up a beer to drown his sorrows, but how could he? Someone had to keep their wits about them in his house. His wife, Willow, had become best friends with the gin bottle to begin with, something to numb the pain, but since she'd agreed to see Vic, the twins' therapist, she'd turned a corner.

She'd never be the same as before, neither would Terry, but they were going in the right direction. It was a direction he felt guilty about, though. Living their lives when the most important aspect of it was gone…well, it wasn't right, was it. The first time he'd laughed after Summer's death had swamped him with remorse. As had the first time he'd woken up not thinking about her immediately. Vic had told Willow the mind was clever in the way it protected you, healed you, and had posed the question: "Would Summer want you both to be so unhappy?"

No, she wouldn't. So Terry had thrown himself into his new job for George and Greg, a bodyguard of sorts for Martin, the bloke who collected protection money. Terry also visited London Teens in his free time, reading everything on the open forums, desperate to catch a slip-up, a clue that a perverted man prowled. He'd told the police what he was doing, and they'd advised him not to, but it had become an obsession. A crutch to get him through. So long as he didn't speak to any kids privately, he wasn't doing any harm. The trouble was, he suspected everyone, even the girl usernames.

Maybe he should let it go and leave the police to their sting operation. The twins also had someone monitoring the site, a bird called Ineke. She gave up a couple of hours a day, watching, reading. It frustrated the fuck out of Terry that no one, including himself, had picked up on anything suss. Mind you, the police wouldn't reveal details of their operation, and maybe they had someone in their sights. Or, the site being closed down that time might have scared the paedo away. He could have moved on to another place.

The idea of that soured his stomach. A child could be being groomed by that wanker right this second. Who the hell *did* that? There had to be something up with their brains, the tossers who engaged in that kind of thing. It wasn't *normal* for adults to fancy kids.

Terry watched the traffic go by from the passenger seat. Martin drove. Terry liked him. They nattered about all sorts, Martin even going so far as to tell him how he'd become involved with the twins. Terry's opinion had already changed about those two since they'd stepped in to help him and Willow, but they'd grown in his estimation even more once he'd found out the extent they'd gone to for Martin.

Martin had been homeless. An Estate leader had kidnapped him, whipped him, creating what he'd called 'patterns' on Martin's skin. It was all a bit savage to be honest, a warped game, but Martin had come out on the other side, now living in one of the twins' flats. Terry reckoned Martin would always have nightmares about his time in captivity, and he had the utmost respect for him. To endure that and still remain a good person, mentally forgiving the man who'd hurt him so he could move on…

Could Terry do the same?

No, never.

The light had been taken out of his life, and he felt bad about thinking of Summer that way, because at one time, *Willow* had been that light. She'd been his be all and end all, then Summer had come along and changed everything. All right, he loved Willow, always would, but she wasn't the same anymore—*he* wasn't the same— and he'd often thought, in the darkness of their bedroom as he'd stared at the ceiling, whether they could get through this together. Whether their love was strong enough to carry them.

It was no longer the kind of love they'd had in the beginning. He doubted anyone's was, once you'd spent a good few years together, the heady rush of attraction waning. But Willow didn't even turn to him for a cuddle anymore, she turned to Vic for support instead. Perhaps she blamed Terry for what had happened. If he'd been a stronger father, a bit more authoritative, insisting Summer didn't go on her laptop so much, or at least monitoring her on the fucking thing, she might never have met that paedo bastard.

But he reminded himself Willow had equal responsibility. Neither of them had wanted to upset the precarious applecart. Summer had morphed into a recalcitrant teen, moody, snappy, and they'd hadn't wanted to ruffle her feathers. Anything for a quiet life. What was it George had told him before Summer had killed herself? That Terry ought to become a parent, not Summer's friend, basically put his foot down, dish out some rules.

And that was the crux of it. The burden he'd carry. Their shit parenting had caused this. God, the amount of times he'd said, "What if I'd...?" It never changed a damn thing, though—hindsight and rumination only brought you regret and pain. Summer was still dead, and the man who'd shoved her down that dangerous path was still out there, probably doing the same thing to other kids.

Each girl on London Teens had been contacted by the police. Their IP addresses had led the coppers to their home addresses, and everyone had been spoken to, warned about a predator, asked if they'd been told to leave envelopes in bins. None of them had admitted to doing so, and because the private messages were encrypted, there was no proof of any such requests. Even the site owner couldn't see what had been said; only the words on the main forums were there for all to see.

Fucking stupid, in Terry's opinion, to go down the encrypted route. Dangerous when minors were so vulnerable. Something ought to be done there, or maybe it had been and he just didn't know about it. He couldn't expect the police to tell him every little thing. After all, his daughter was dead and didn't need protecting anymore, so why *would* they tell him?

He sighed, annoyed with himself for going over the same old ground. As soon as his mind wasn't busy with other things, it constantly turned to Summer, to that pervert, their chats, which he wished he hadn't read because they scrolled through his mind in the dead of night now. He thought about her hiding herself away in her bedroom during the time she'd been delivering the envelopes, and after, when she'd worried so much about the bastard putting her images on social media anyway, despite her doing what he'd asked.

He remembered being a teenager, where everything seemed magnified and so much worse than it really was. Not to downplay what Summer had gone through, but if only she'd known it could so easily have been fixed. Terry and Willow would have moved away from the area if it had made her feel safer. They'd have done anything, even let her dye her hair if the pics had shown up on Instagram and Facebook, anything so she wasn't recognised.

As for the suicide note…

Jesus Christ, that had been a hard read. She'd thanked them for being the best parents, for the life they'd given her, and told them not to blame themselves. She'd wished she could have talked to them about the shame she'd felt, but the embarrassment of it had prevented her from saying anything so deep. And she'd said sorry — for leaving them, causing them grief.

Terry swiped at his eyes.

"You okay, mate?" Martin asked.

"So-so."

"Do you want to talk about her?"

Martin was too perceptive.

"Nah." Terry smiled, a sad one. Summer was more like him than he'd realised. She'd kept shit to herself, too, instead of talking it through. "Maybe it's time I give in, go and see Vic. He's helped Willow no end."

"Therapy is good."

"It's all a bit American, though, know what I mean? The only time people saw a therapist when I was a kid was because they were mental. You know, it meant the men in white coats would come along."

"Not sure about the term mental in the way you said it. It's not very nice, is it."

"And that's another thing, we can't say fuck all these days before the snowflakes start piping up. Don't tell me you're one of *those* people."

"No, but I think being mindful of what might upset someone isn't a bad thing."

"I get that, but to *this* degree? Where I can't say someone's mental?"

Martin shrugged.

Prior to losing his child, Terry would have still gone at it, putting his point across until he'd got Martin to agree with him, but these days he understood that what *he* believed wasn't necessarily the right thing. Not to mention the twins would have his arse on a plate if he upset Martin. They treated him like their little brother, and Terry was fucked if he'd step on any toes there.

It was weird, discovering things about himself, seeing who he was as if from the outside. He didn't like half of what he saw. If he met himself on the street, he'd think he was a right knob. He now understood why other people had called him that in the past. He presented as a bolshy arsewipe, perhaps a defence mechanism from when he'd been a kid, struggling to fit in, to find an identity. He'd been so quiet until he'd discovered that being loud got you noticed.

Maybe he ought to revert to who he used to be up until he'd been around eight. Then he'd been the silent one, the one who didn't garner attention. Perhaps he wouldn't have to suffer with people staring at him then as if he must have known Summer was being groomed.

Those types of looks killed him every time.

"What shall we talk about, then?" he asked, needing Martin to take over before he spiralled and went into one of his foul moods. Sometimes, making decisions was too hard, too much.

"Whatever you like." Martin smiled. "Apart from the snowflake thing."

Terry's mind went blank. He couldn't think of a damn thing to say. Would that happen if he sat on Vic's sofa? Would he clam up?

Saved by the view ahead, Terry stiffened. They drew up to a corner shop, an altercation going on outside. He rolled his shoulders. Now *this* would take his mind off shit. He unclipped his seat belt and got out, marching towards two people having a barney: Ivory Reynolds and Marnie Fields.

"What the fuck's going on?" he barked.

"Piss off, Terry, this is fuck all to do with you," Ivory snapped.

"It's everything to do with me when you're rowing outside a shop the twins protect."

Marnie planted her hands on her hips. "What, you're working for *them* now?"

"Yeah, so move it along."

Ivory turned to Marnie. "Watch your back, you fucking little cow. If you so much as *breathe* near my husband again, I'll have you." She strutted off.

Marnie called after her, "If you were servicing him right, he wouldn't have come to me, would he? Your fanny's got cobwebs, so I heard!"

Ivory held her middle finger up. She kept going but said, "He'll be nice at first, then see what you get… It takes a strong woman to put up with it, and that's not you."

Terry shook his head at Marnie. "I wouldn't mess with her if I were you. She's well angry."

Marnie stared at him. "Why don't you piss off and mind your own business?"

"I can get you banned from this shop, so less of the lip."

She smirked. "Christ, your kid dies and you think you can do and say whatever you like? Mind you, there's no change there, you've always been an arsehole."

She swanned off, and it was a fucking good job an' all. Her mentioning Summer in such a crass way had ignited his anger, and he'd had to stop himself from punching her in the face. It reminded him of when he'd thumped Paula in the stomach, the receptionist at the factory he'd got the sack from. He'd found out that Cod, some old pervert, had accessed London Teens. Terry had convinced himself that Cod was the bloke Summer had been talking to. His frustration at no one believing the old man was a paedo had bubbled over, and when he'd gone to find out why his last wages hadn't been paid, he'd taken it out on Paula. He'd never hit a woman before her, and he'd vowed to never do it again, yet he'd just come so close.

The twins had killed Cod, disposed of his body, and Terry had reveled in his death. Pictured it over and over again.

Yeah, he needed to go and see Vic. Get himself sorted. The way he imagined every paedo being castrated wasn't good for his mindset.

Martin came up beside him. "Come on."

They entered the shop, Terry annoyed with himself for getting rattled so quickly at Marnie. Maybe that was his life now, a series of events that would test him to see if he struck out again. The anger and despair at Summer's death had to go somewhere, but he worried it would be directed at the wrong people. He walked such a thin line these days, so desperate to make that envelope man pay. Now, if he could just get his hands on the fucker, he'd have an outlet. Months had passed, no sign of the man being caught, and it frustrated the hell out of him.

One day he'd be found, though. And Terry would be standing at the front of the queue to beat the shite out of him. Whoever that cunt was, he didn't deserve to live, and Terry had no problem killing him and going down for it.

Justice had to be done, no matter the consequences.

Chapter Five

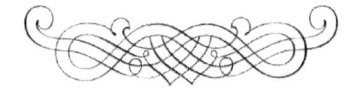

Prison wasn't somewhere Anaisha wanted to be, but it was the only way to get answers. As she was over sixteen, she could come here alone, although she'd had to apply for a provisional driving licence to show proof of identity. It had surprised her that Shaq had agreed to her request for a visiting order. Maybe he saw it as an opportunity to taunt her instead of

Dayton. She wouldn't put it past him. If he hadn't been seen and caught, would he have come for her next? Would Mum and Dad be childless by now?

The thought gave her chills.

It had become a big responsibility, making up for them now only having one kid. She'd found herself trying to be herself and *Dayton all rolled into one. Telling his silly jokes, patting Mum on the top of her arm when she went past her, like her brother had always done. Doing the washing up after dinner in his stead, without fail, because he'd hated seeing Mum standing there doing it after a long day's work. He'd sent her to the living room to sit with Dad so they could have a moment together. Always thoughtful, always so bloody kind.*

Anaisha wasn't kind anymore. Something had happened to her since his death. On the outside, she seemed the same, albeit dogged by the shadows of grief, but inside... So much hate festered, and she found herself wanting to lash out at Shaq, teach him a lesson. To dish out payback.

He consumed her thoughts, as did becoming a police officer. On the flip side of wanting to be mean, she wanted to help others like Dayton, to prove people didn't need to be arrested because they were black, or taunted, bullied, stabbed. It had become an obsession, as had wanting to hear the word 'sorry' coming from Shaq's mouth.

How she'd feel when she saw the bastard again, she wasn't sure, but she'd soon find out because the door ahead opened and an officer beckoned for the queue of people to file into the visiting hall. Anaisha had looked this place up online and viewed images of the visiting room, so at least she had some clue what she'd be walking into. Nauseated, she trundled along behind the people in front of her and steeled herself for finding out Shaq had tricked her and he wasn't sitting there at all.

What greeted her were no prisoners and a lot of tables and chairs that reminded her of being at school. A hatch in the wall already had a line in front of it, and two men behind a counter served drinks, cakes, and crisps. Anaisha tagged onto the end of it, wondering if the blokes were prisoners. Maybe some goodies would help to sweeten Shaq, make him think she was nice and wanted to be friends so something good came out of this mess. She could pretend to be kind to him if it got her result she craved. An apology.

But she didn't want to make friends, and she wasn't nice. And he'd pay for what he'd done.

She bought him a coffee and a selection of cakes, a cup of tea for herself. There was no way she could eat, not with her stomach churning. She found a free table, placed the tray on it, then took off the polystyrene cups and paper plates of food. She returned the tray to the hatch—a sign instructed everyone to do that. Maybe trays became a weapon in the wrong hands.

She went to the table and sat. No time to stew. A door opened, and inmates poured in, all in identical clothes—sweatshirts and jogging bottoms. The second Shaq spotted her he grinned, his posture loose, and he came over to the table casually. In his shoes she'd be nervous. Facing the sister of the person you'd killed was supposed to be daunting, you were meant to show remorse, but it was clear he didn't feel anything but smug. He sat, lounging, and stared right at her.

"Why did you let me come?" she asked.

"Why not? It's not like I can bully people in here without someone retaliating, is it. You'll give me that fix I need."

"Not if I don't come back again."

"But you will. You're one of those types who want to reform me, make me see the 'error of my ways'." He created air quotes with his long fingers.

Fingers that had curled around the handle of a knife.

He was so wrong about her. She had the need to see him suffer, to hurt him, kill him. Several times since Dayton's death she'd imagined Shaq getting ill, cancer or something eating him alive. A horrible, wicked thought, but she'd found grief, for her, had come bearing the gift of malevolence, and if she wasn't careful, it was going to twist her up into someone unrecognisable.

"*I just want you to say sorry so I can pass it on to my mum and dad.*"

"*You have to be sorry to say it, and I'm not.*"

"*So you don't feel bad even a little bit?*"

"*Nope. He had it coming.*"

"*Why? What did he ever do to you?*"

He eyed the cakes. "Are these to soften me up?"

"*I thought…I mean, you won't be getting much of this in here, will you? It's a treat, something nice.*"

"*Why the* fuck *would you want to do something nice for me?*"

She shrugged. "The world is full of enough hate as it is."

"*You're fucked in the head. How can you sit here with the man who killed your brother and yap on about forgiveness—what, are you saying you forgive* me? *You need to get your priorities straight. You're meant to see me as scum, hate me, want me to burn in Hell.*"

I do, but you're never going to know that until the last knockings. "*Dayton wouldn't want me to be bitter. Even when you bullied him, he still said you must have issues to behave like that and we should cut you some slack. He was so much older than you, and he saw you as a child who needed help."*

Shaq let out a "pfft" then grabbed a cupcake. "A regular do-gooder like you, was he?"

"He was someone with compassion who was able to read between the lines. Was he right? Do you have issues? I don't even know why I'm asking because I know you do. Why, though? Why is him—and me— not being pure such a big thing for you? Shit like that isn't in a person until they're taught it."

"Shut your mouth."

She'd hit a nerve, and her stab in the dark had found the right reason for his behaviour. "Are your parents radicals or something? Like Hitler with his Aryan bullshit?"

"Don't talk to me about them." He busied himself eating the cake.

Anaisha picked up her tea and sipped while he munched through everything she'd bought. He stared at her the whole time. Prior to Dayton's murder she'd have been afraid, worried he might hit her or spew his vile views, but nothing could touch her now. Nothing was worse than losing her brother—except losing her parents—so he could throw whatever he liked at her.

She wanted that apology, and for as long as he'd allow her to come here, she'd come. There was no way she could shut off her thoughts until he'd paid for what he'd done. Like how, right this second, she wished she held a knife so she could slice that smug grin off his face. Pierce him in the eyes so he couldn't see her pain. Cut out his tongue so he couldn't taste those fucking cakes.

He reached for his coffee. "Whatever you're here for, it's not going to work. There's too much damage been done."

Was that a speck of remorse? Was it his way of acknowledging the damage he'd done to Anaisha and her parents? To Dayton? She'd need specific words, clear and concise, ones that said it explicitly, so there was no room for confusion.

"There has," *she agreed,* "but there's always time to repent."

"Fucking hell, did you find God or something?"

"No. If there was a God, no one would be cruel. No one would become fucked-up enough to stab someone on the street—or even want to. My brother wouldn't be dead."

He stared at her. "That damage. Just so you know, so we're clear, I wasn't talking about him dying and the fallout. I was talking about me."

He got up and walked towards the exit, leaving her pondering what the hell he'd meant. He was damaged, everyone knew that, but would he ever tell her why?

Chapter Six

Bryan Flint sat with Anaisha in the staffroom, annoyed Janine had sent her to talk to him. He didn't have it in him to chat about his rise up the police ladder. He hadn't found a place he could prowl online to settle his anxiety and found it increasingly difficult to maintain the façade that he was a happy-go-lucky man at work. Being so with Anaisha was proving too much. Still, he'd got himself into this situation, and it wasn't her fault he was a tetchy bastard inside.

He'd steered clear of London Teens ever since it had closed for that fortnight of investigations, and fucking hell, it was hard to stay away. The place was like a drug, calling to him, but he'd managed it. He had a brand-new laptop he didn't want to infect with his former life. He'd given up that line of making money, the photos of girls he used to sell, cutting all associations with his customers and closing his dark-web image site and bank account. Better to wipe the slate clean and pretend he hadn't been a pervert. That he hadn't been Fishy_For_Life, amongst other usernames.

The twins paid him a fair whack each week, even when they didn't need him for anything. A retainer they called it, but it was nowhere near the cash the pictures had generated. He missed the process of what he used to do. How he'd spoken to girls as if he were a kid himself, making them trust him, them sending innocent pictures that soon turned to rude ones, then he dished out the instructions to leave small amounts of cash in envelopes for him to collect out of the bins they were placed in. That was the bit he loved best, the control, frightening them, taking the risk of grabbing the money, and it had been taken away from him because of Summer's death. The stupid little cow had let it all get inside her head, and she hadn't been able to handle the pressure.

That had been the warning he'd needed, really. To step away, pack it in. He'd be a fool to set up his scam elsewhere, so he just needed something that would fill the void. What, though? What else would give him that thrill?

"So what are you working on at the minute that's made you want to be a detective?" he asked as a way to make Anaisha think he was actually interested in what she had to say.

"Trying to find the bastard who made Summer Meeks kill herself."

That snagged his attention good and proper. Here was the perfect opportunity to get on the inside, to know what the team were up to. It had been worrying him that they'd discover it was him, even though he'd used a VPN and destroyed his perv laptop. It had been months, though, and he hadn't heard any whispers about the perpetrator being traced and watched, yet still he fretted. As a police officer, he knew full well how investigations could take a long time.

"No news on who the bloke is, then?" He sipped his coffee then opened a Snickers.

"No. Bloody VPNs should be banned. It's a known one, used widely, so he didn't even have the sense to choose one that was completely hidden, but we don't know where it originates, who owns the site."

Flint hadn't bristled at her comment, the one basically saying he was thick as pig shit because he'd chosen a well-used VPN service, but he *had* done his homework before he'd chosen it. It may well be on a known list that showed someone wanted to get online without being detected, but at no point had the company owner's identity been discovered prior to Flint using it. People who ran those kinds of sites were clever and knew exactly how to disguise who they were. Flint reckoned he was safe, but it still gave him the willies that some loophole or other would crop up and the team Anaisha was on would discover more.

"So what are you doing, then? Just sitting on the site waiting to see who says something dodgy?"

She explained she had a username and that she currently spoke to one of the VPN users, a male claiming to be sixteen. Someone else had chatted to the second user, but whoever it was hadn't acted strange, and when asked where they lived, they'd given their address and real name. That user was a fourteen-year-old boy, and officers had been round to double-check.

"I've got a feeling the one I'm talking to isn't a man either, that he really is a boy like the other one," she said. "I called him out today about the picture he sent me of himself. It's from a stock site, and he said it's his account, that he uploads images to sell."

This was all too close to the bone. Had she said that to try and trip him up? Did her team know *he* was the pervert who'd sold pictures and they were just waiting to catch him out? Was that the real reason Janine had sent Anaisha his way? His heart rate scattered. That upload comment had shit him up, and he felt sick, especially is Janine was in the know on this case. Christ, had she informed the twins?

Anaisha sighed. "Makes sense as he's a photographer, or so he says. I don't know, it all seems off. One, I'm an adult potentially talking to a kid, which is icky, and two, I'm meeting him tomorrow at the cinema. *I* feel the like the fucking pervert."

Flint settled a bit at her words, then reminded himself she might have said *that* on purpose, too. "If it's a boy...God, all that hard work, wasted."

"I know."

"So what kind of thing did that man say to Summer? Is it similar to the person you're chatting with?"

"Who, Fishy?"

He feigned confusion. "What the hell's fishy?"

"The username of the one Summer was involved with. Fishy_For_Life."

"Ah right."

"But to answer your question, their approaches aren't the same, unless Fishy's now behaving differently because of Summer's death."

"What do you mean?"

"Well, Fishy was an outright perv to her. He didn't take long to ask for dirty pictures, and some of the stuff he said... Gross."

That was a lie. Flint had laid the groundwork well enough, and for long enough, or so he'd thought, and he hadn't been *that* gross, had he?

Now he'd dumped the laptop, he couldn't go to the files he'd created and read the conversations to see.

"Gross compared to Amateur anyway," she added. "He hasn't asked for anything rude in all this time. I've got this feeling he isn't Summer's man. Still, we'll soon find out tomorrow if the kid doesn't show up."

"Ah, but he could get cold feet. How old is the girl you're pretending to be?"

"Thirteen."

"You said he's sixteen. He might be worried about the age gap, getting in trouble for chatting to a minor."

"Oliver said the same thing."

"So are you nattering to him outside of work as well?"

"Yes, on a burner phone. It'd look weird if I didn't talk in the evenings. He might twig something's up if I just kept it to work hours."

"What time are you meeting him?"

"Half one at the Odeon on Bridgegate Street. Oliver and the team are going with me."

"What's the plan? If there isn't a kid who looks like the photo he sent, it could be anyone. How will you even know who to approach?"

"Oliver's briefing how it'll go in the morning, but I'm wondering if he'll get me to send messages when we're there so they can see who picks up their phone."

"If you're meant to be thirteen, and it's actually a bloke, he's going to recognise you if you don't look much different to when you were a teenager. He's going to clock that it's a sting and he'll just fuck off."

Anaisha stared at the Snickers he hadn't eaten. "Between me and you, it all seems a bit disorganised."

"I agree. If he doesn't answer your messages outside the Odeon tomorrow, unless he walks off and it's obvious he's suss, none of you will know who he is. If it were me and I spotted you, knew I'd been set up, I'd go inside to watch a film. Then he'll probably abandon your chat and start a new one with another girl." Flint needed information so probed with: "Is there any way you can tell which username is using the VPN?"

"Yes, the site owner can see which username it is, just not where he is."

"Well, here's hoping it's a kid, which means Summer's pervert has stopped going on London Teens. Unless he's now ditched using a VPN, which would be bloody daft if he doesn't want to get caught. I expect your team are monitoring all the IPs, yes?"

"Yep."

"Good luck with it anyway." He bit into his Snickers.

"I reckon it's all going to go tits up."

For you maybe, but not for me. You've given me all the information I need.

Chapter Seven

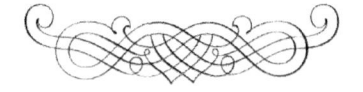

Ivory Reynolds had been brave earlier—on the outside. On the inside, she'd shit bricks confronting Marnie like that. It was so out of character for her, but she'd had to save face, pretend she cared what her husband was up to. Whispers in the school playground had reached Ivory. Kendall had been dipping his wick elsewhere, and Marnie hadn't even denied it. And it was true what Marnie had said. Ivory's fanny *did* have metaphorical cobwebs. Kendall hadn't forced himself on her for a while, and she was thankful for it, but how dare he think it was okay to piss about behind her back? Just one more thing in the long list of crap he put her through.

She was sick of him, and if she were a decent mother, she'd have taken their little boy away from such a toxic household long before now, but she *wasn't* decent, she was still there, and she hated herself for being so weak. Why couldn't she stand up to him like she'd done with Marnie?

Because he'll belt me for it, that's why.

In the women's magazines Mum passed on to her every Saturday after she was finished with them, there were plenty of articles that stated people in domestic violence relationships found it difficult—and scary—to walk away. Apparently, the most dangerous time was the point the abused left. She didn't plan to go to Mum's when she got up the courage to fuck off. Kendall would go straight there, and he'd talk to Ivory out of earshot, threatening her, saying she had to go home or he'd kidnap their son.

He loved saying stuff like that.

It was all a bit of a mess. Mum didn't know who Kendall really was beneath the façade. Ivory had hidden it, not wanting the 'I told you so' to come flying her way. Mum had said, back in the early days, that there was 'something about Kendall' she couldn't put her finger on. Ivory hadn't seen it at the time, of course she hadn't, she'd been young and head over heels, sucked in by his charm. But he'd changed as soon as Remy had been born. He had Ivory over a barrel, or so he thought, but she *was* in the process of leaving him—leaving every single thing she owned behind, too, apart from her child.

She'd reached out and found help. While Remy was at school, she'd walked into the Social Services building in a sudden burst of courage and told them everything. A caseworker had been assigned, and she'd informed Ivory that a new refuge had opened not long ago, Dolly's Haven, and as soon as she felt safe enough to go there, a place would be waiting. The trouble was, Kendall popped home unexpectedly—a lot—and he'd said his friends spied on her. He wasn't lying, otherwise, how would he know she'd visited the market or town at certain times? Or that she'd gone to the doctor's surgery? Before he'd had a chance to mention her visit to the social, she'd admitted to being there, claiming she'd applied for a job as a cleaner in the building. He'd seemed to accept that and be pleased she'd volunteered the information without being prompted. He'd probably congratulated himself on successfully managing to indoctrinate her.

But she wasn't so indoctrinated that she didn't know her arse from her elbow. She knew damn well she shouldn't be with him and that what he did to her and Remy was abhorrent.

Now, she just had the dilemma of *when* to run. Her caseworker had offered to come and pick her up, but with Ivory being watched, that wasn't wise. What if one of Kendall's mates saw the car and followed it to Haven? Ivory had been given the address, and it didn't make sense, because that big house belonged to some old boy who never ventured outside. Yvonne, the woman behind the counter at the shop, had mentioned it when Ivory had nipped in there for the bread she hadn't bothered buying earlier, what with Marnie starting on her as soon as she'd spotted her. The social worker had said Haven's whereabouts should never be spoken about to anyone, it had to remain a secret, secure place. Did Yvonne know about it and that's why she'd spouted lies about the old man living there? Why would she even know it was a refuge, though? Was she a battered woman ready to leave her fella, too?

Ivory left the house, walking back to the shop, not only to collect the bread but to have a word with Yvonne. There was no way she'd take her son to a house owned by some ancient bloke, staying there with him, no matter whether he was kind and had opened up his home for people like her. It felt well off.

She entered the shop. Yvonne wasn't behind the counter and no other customers were in, so Ivory grabbed a cheap and cheerful loaf then found her stacking chocolate down one of the aisles.

Yvonne glanced across at her. "Back again? I won't be a sec."

"That old boy you said about, the one in the big house. Why did you even tell me about it?"

Yvonne put a Mars on a stack then folded her arms. "It gives me something to talk about. Everyone's gossiping about it, so I thought you'd want to know, too. I didn't get the chance to tell you before because Marnie stuck her oar in, but some reckon it's a singer. He's retired now. Can't for the life of me remember his bloody name, though."

Ivory frowned. Was that a rumour as a cover for Haven? If it was, how stupid, because people would get nosy and go there, trying to catch a glimpse of him. Or was Haven next door? Fucking hell, Ivory hated not being able to mention the refuge in order to find out what she needed to know. If she did, Yvonne might let it slip to Kendall next time he was in here for his booze and fags, then he'd know exactly where to find her.

Yvonne wandered towards the counter, calling over her shoulder, "I remember when that was all just wasteland. People are saying it's millionaire's row down there now. Six massive houses, there is."

That answered one question, so Yvonne must have got confused as to which house the singer actually lived in.

Ivory joined her at the counter and paid for the bread. "Does anyone really care about an old singer, though?"

"Nah, he was never liked much anyway, not after those rumours about kiddies, like that bloody Jimmy Saville, if you catch my drift."

"Jesus."

"It's just something to talk about, that's all. Anyway, there's no point going to have a gander because there are cameras, and anyone found outside the walls will be arrested if they don't bog off."

"How do you know?"

"George told me. He said some security blokes stand outside in shifts. Bloody boring job if you ask me. I bet the old boy knows he needs protecting from vigilantes. Loads of people online reckon he lied his way out of any paedo charges, so it stands to reason they'd want to go round there and lop his dick off."

The more Ivory thought about it, the more she reckoned no old man lived there. What Yvonne had said pointed to the house being Haven. Security would be there to protect the people living inside. "How come George knows so much about it?"

Yvonne rolled her eyes. "Because he's *George*. The Brothers know everything. If there's a kiddie fiddler on their Estate, they're going to be aware, or at least I'd like to think they are. Still, some of them don't exactly advertise who they are, do they?"

Ivory nodded. "Hmm. Well, I'd better be off."

She picked up the loaf and walked out, her mind going like the clappers. She didn't want to risk going back to the Social Services building to ask whether it was truly safe to go to Haven, someone could be watching her, and besides, she had to pick Remy up from school soon. She didn't dare use her phone to ring her caseworker; even if she deleted the call log or any messages, Kendall always knew who she'd rung or texted. He must have put some sort of spyware on her phone. That was likely another reason how he knew where she was all the time.

She'd be leaving the mobile behind when she left him.

How could she get hold of the twins? Who could she ask without arousing suspicion and having some sneaky little twat running to Kendall with tales about her?

She checked her phone for the time. She had an hour before she needed to be at the school. The Angel was on the way there, so if she nipped home to drop the bread off, she could pop into the pub. Debbie, the woman who owned it, was rumoured to be good friends with The Brothers.

Would she help? But what excuse could Ivory give Kendall if she was seen going inside?

I'll say I applied for another cleaning job.

God, she hated having to think up excuses for everything so she didn't rock the boat. Living on her nerves had become second nature, but lately, her anxiety had got so bad she'd had panic attacks at work, so often that she'd been 'let go'. Add to that the hassle of trying to find another job, Kendall always banging on about them being 'poor' now with only his wage coming in, and she needed a complete reset.

Running away was no longer a dream. For Remy's sake, she was going to make it a reality. If she left now, as he was only little, he might forget the life they'd led with his father. Or were some things so ingrained in his head that he'd always remember them? Would it affect him as an adult? Would he become one of the broken who committed crime?

Shit, I need shooting for what I've allowed to happen.

At home, she put the bread on the worktop and rushed back out. Sensing eyes on her, she moved casually, slowly, as if she was taking a gentle walk to the school. Mum used to pick

Remy up when Ivory worked, and it was nice to actually be able to do it herself. Spend more time with him before Kendall came home.

She arrived at The Angel and went inside without hesitating to look over her shoulder at who could be following her. She approached the bar, and a woman came over to her, LISA on her name badge.

"Hi, is Debbie in?" Ivory asked quietly.

"No, but I can get hold of her for you." Lisa frowned and stared past Ivory. She leaned forward and asked, "Is everything okay? Do you need to speak to me in private?"

Ivory nodded, relieved. Her follower must have come in after her, Lisa spotting him or her. She lifted the bar hatch and led the way towards double doors with a TOILETS plaque above them. She took Ivory down a corridor and looked up at a camera above a door. A buzz sounded, and she walked into what appeared to be a reception area.

This must be the massage parlour people go on about.

An older woman sat behind the counter filing her nails. "Oh! I didn't know a new girl was starting…"

Lisa shook her head. "She isn't." She turned to Ivory. "This is Amaryllis. Anything you say is fine in front of her. She knows how to keep a secret. What's up? Why did it look like some bloke was following you?"

It all spilled out in a babble: Kendall, her need to run, the caseworker telling her about Haven, the old man recluse, being watched and tailed everywhere, needing a new job, Marnie, all of it.

"Fucking hell," Amaryllis said. "You can't live like that. I'll get hold of The Brothers, shall I?"

Lisa nodded. "I think that's best. Where are you going after here?"

Ivory swallowed and wiped the tears off her face. "I have to get my son from school."

"Do that then come back. I'll say something loudly when we go into the pub so whoever that bloke is will hear it. Stand at the bar." She squeezed Ivory's upper arm. "It'll be all right now, okay?"

Ivory nodded and went with Lisa. Entering the pub, she glanced around, her heart skipping a beat; she spotted one of Kendall's friends drinking a pint. He smiled at her, smug. God, she hated him for doing whatever Kendall said, thinking it was okay to spy on her. She stood a couple of metres away from him, so *angry* at being watched, and waited for Lisa to go behind the bar.

"Right, I'm happy with your CV, so if you could nip in once you've picked up your son to fill out the paperwork, the job's yours."

"Thank you," Ivory said, and it felt like this was a film, her playing a part. She wasn't really going to get out of her horrible life and start a new one—good things like that didn't happen to her anymore. "I'll see you in a bit."

She walked past Kendall's mate, who texted on his phone, likely reporting back to her husband. Outside, she took a deep breath, and at the end of the street, she peeked back. He wasn't following her this time. He'd probably been told to wait until she returned—or Kendall himself would be there, ready to berate her for taking their son into a pub.

She collected Remy who was as subdued as he always was these days. His teacher had said on more than one occasion that he was happy in class, so Ivory could only surmise it was the thought of going home that sent his mood dark.

Poor kid. I should have left a long time ago. Look what I've put him through.

She was dying to tell him the news, that they'd never be going home again if she had her way. The Brothers would be at the pub when they got there, and they'd take care of everything, wouldn't they?

Despite her fake-happy chatter, Remy didn't respond.

"We've just got to pop in here for a bit, okay?" She pushed open the door to The Angel, shitting herself in case Kendall was there and he insisted on taking Remy away from her.

His mate still stood at the bar.

Lisa smiled. "Hi! Come through, and we'll get that paperwork sorted. Is the littlun allowed some crisps?"

Ivory nodded and, once Lisa had grabbed some cheese and onion, Ivory once again trotted after her into reception. Amaryllis pointed to one of the doors, and Lisa opened it, ushering Ivory and Remy inside.

Oh fuck. Oh God. The twins were here, and they were so bloody massive up close it took her breath away for a moment. In their grey suits, white shirts, and red ties, they stood in front of a sofa, and one of them gestured to the other couch.

Ivory sat, Remy perching beside her and taking the crisps from Lisa shyly.

Lisa left, closing the door.

Ivory's armpits went clammy, and sweat beaded above her top lip. She dabbed it away, nervous. Would they ask her if she wanted Kendall 'sorted'? Would he be given a Cheshire? Rumours flew around about those, that George loved slicing people's faces, but maybe it was just Chinese whispers.

The twins sat.

"George," one of them said and then pointed to the other. "Greg. We got the gist off Amaryllis. Are you one hundred percent ready?"

Grateful he wasn't saying things outright in front of her boy, Ivory nodded. "I can't…he…"

"Yep, we can imagine." George smiled at Remy. "All right, son?"

Remy looked over at him then lowered his gaze.

Ivory opened his crisps. "He's…"

"…understandably quiet," George finished. "He'll be fine soon. Different kid. Someone's joining our team next week, a teacher, so he won't miss out on anything. Best there's no school for a while, eh? We've brought our van. You can get in the back so you're not seen. Leave your phone switched off here; Sharon at Haven will give you another one. I presume you'll want to let your mum know you're okay—you can use the special burner we have for those types of calls. Obviously, don't tell her where we've taken you."

He went on to explain the rules, and although he did it gently, there was still a warning in his tone. It was clear he felt passionate about keeping anyone living at Haven safe, and if someone fucked that up, the result wouldn't be pretty.

Ivory would agree to anything so long as they helped her. "There's this woman he's been seeing. Marnie Fields. He might…you know, do the same thing to her. We've never got on, but I wouldn't want her going through what I have. Do you know her?"

"Yeah. We'll sort it."

George tried to engage with Remy again, only getting a response when he asked what his favourite present would be if he could have anything he wanted.

"A bike," Remy said quietly, "because me dad broke mine. He threw it at the wall in our garden, and the front wheel twisted."

Greg took a phone out and prodded the screen.

"Then we'll get you a new one. My brother's looking into it right now, see?" George took a deep breath as if digesting what Remy had said—he acted as if he wanted to rip Kendall a new one. "Do you like your dad?"

"Nah, he hurts me mum and smacks me and stuff."

"Would you like to live somewhere else?"

For the first time, Remy lit up. "Yeah." Then he sagged. "But we can't, because me dad said we're not allowed to go nowhere without him."

"You are allowed." George took the phone off Greg and turned it round to face Remy. "What about that bike, eh?"

Remy's mouth downturned. "Dad will break that an' all."

"No he won't, because you're going to live somewhere he can't find you, and then he's going to go on a trip and won't come back." George eyed Ivory.

Fucking hell, they're going to kill him?

George nodded at her, then turned back to Remy. "There's a big garden, and you'll be able to ride round and round. I expect the bike will be there when we arrive because one of our friends called Will is going to buy it in a minute. What do you think about that?"

"We haven't got no stuff with us."

"You don't need it. We'll buy you clothes and whatever. Lots of toys, and a teddy bear is waiting for you. Would that be good?"

"Yeah."

Remy didn't seem convinced, and Ivory struggled with her emotions. Gratitude was uppermost, but a sense of doom lay beneath it.

"Will he find us?" she whispered.

"Nope. We'll discuss things once we get there. There's a little girl Remy can play with while we talk." George stood. "Come on, buster. Let's go and see your new bike."

They all filed out of the room.

Ivory couldn't see for the tears.

Chapter Eight

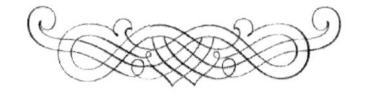

Shaq fucking hated it in here, but it was the best place for him. If he opened his mouth and said some of the shit he'd said to Dayton, he'd find himself shanked. Prison meant he had to put up and shut up. It meant he couldn't hurt anyone else. It meant Anaisha was safe.

No one would understand his reasoning, just like they hadn't understood his former beliefs—beliefs that still popped into his head and tried to turn him back into the bastard he'd been, where he had visions of hurting Anaisha. It was a constant battle every day to keep the whispers out.

God, he sounded mental, and maybe he was.

For the past few months, he'd had plenty of time to think. His cluttered, overfull mind had some clarity inside it now. When you were bombarded with negativity, when someone in your life was so adept at convincing you their mantra was the right one, you ended up believing it if you weren't strong enough.

Children weren't strong enough. He couldn't even remember the first time those views had been expressed to him, but he'd been little, he knew that much. It felt as though they'd always been there, inside him, something he'd been born thinking. Anaisha saying the opposite on her first visit, that he'd been taught—fucking hell, she'd hit the nail on the head, the perceptive cow. He'd been indoctrinated, and off he'd gone, out on the streets, spitting out all the words that had been pumped into his mind and soul. And he'd thought he was right, that the teacher was right, even though he knew damn well, deep down, that they were wrong.

Jesus, it was all so fucked-up.

He couldn't look Mum in the eye whenever she visited. She had so many questions every time, so much she wanted to understand, and she demanded answers he couldn't give her, because the teacher had warned him not to say anything. He'd threatened him.

She sat opposite him now, a paper plate of cupcakes between them, and it reminded him of Anaisha and how she always made sure he was sugared up when she came here. Kindness, it reminded him of that an' all, how some people could be so nice, even to the vilest of people.

He didn't deserve nice.

"Make me understand," Mum said. "How could you say and think the things you do? I mean, look at me."

He did. At her white skin, her blue eyes, her blonde hair. He loved her—she'd taken care of him, given him her all, despite him being an arsehole to her with no explanation. Yet he hated her, too—she'd married a black man, and that was so wrong. They'd made him, and he wasn't pure.

But it was also right. Now he'd had time to view them through a different lens, he saw his parents were the salt of the earth, fucking good people, made for each other. Yet the teacher had told him they'd made a mistake, that even though they were in love, they should never have got together. The two sides of the argument clashed in his mind a lot lately, now he was separated from him. It was as if without having that pecking voice in his ear, reminding him of the 'truth', or how it was 'supposed' to be, he'd been able to see things from the other side.

The problem with that was, it shone a light on how horrible Shaq had been. That light stung his eyes — he'd never admit it was anything else, like emotion, or guilt, or remorse. He had to maintain the ruse that he was still that bastard. If he didn't, bad shit would happen.

Sometimes, he preferred the days when he'd believed the teacher, when nothing could have swayed him from the belief that whites should stick with whites, blacks with blacks. In those days before prison, and for a month or so afterwards, he'd still felt the same. But regret at treating Mum like shit and never telling her why, it ate at him in the long, boring days with nothing much to do except think. She thought he disliked her as a person, held some grudge, but that wasn't true. If only she looked like Dad, he'd have been fine with her. If only the teacher hadn't piped up, Shaq wouldn't have behaved as he had. Yes, he'd have naturally learned that some people frowned on a black-

and-white union, that the kids produced from that went through some crap, but it wouldn't have messed him up to the degree it had.

"What did I ever do to you to make you hate me so much?" Mum asked. "You were fine until you were about six, then you changed. I've never smacked you, never treated you badly. I'm struggling with it all." *She paused. "I know what you said in your defence when you were sentenced, why you killed that poor man, but he was just like you, so I don't get it. How can you blame someone for having a white mum when you have one yourself?"*

"You wouldn't understand." The teacher will kill me if I tell.

But would he, though? How could he when Shaq was in here and the teacher was out there? Unless he was as well-connected as he'd said and he could make anything happen. Christ, he might know people in here for all Shaq knew, people who'd murder him.

If Shaq opened up to Mum, told her everything, it would hurt her so much. He'd already done enough damage. Better to let her think he disliked her because she was white rather than tell her the truth. The truth would destroy her, especially because she thought the teacher was a good and honest man, a kind man, someone she trusted. Shaq doubted she'd believe him anyway. She'd defend the teacher, wouldn't be able to comprehend that he was a sick motherfucker who'd twisted her son up.

"I love you," he said, needing her to know that. "I know you won't get it, and if I could turn the clock back to a time when I didn't see your skin colour, I would, but too much has happened, there's too much in here." He tapped the side of his head.

He hated having to make out he still believed what he'd been taught. But if he didn't, the teacher would find out. Mum would likely repeat her conversations with him, and Shaq couldn't risk him finding out.

"What the hell happened to you?" she whispered with a shake of her head, as though she couldn't believe what her son had become.

"I can't tell you that. Just leave it, all right?"

She nodded but at least looked relieved that he loved her. That was something she could carry around with her when she walked out of here. It couldn't be helped that he was leaving her in confusion and she'd likely sit there every night with Dad, talking through everything so she could make sense of it.

The teacher would also kill Dad if Shaq told on him.

"Life is shit and then you die," he said randomly.

"What? Oh God, I feel like I don't know you."

"You don't. I've done things, and will continue to do things to protect you. It doesn't seem like it, but I swear, this is all for you and Dad."

How could he open his mouth and let it all spill out when the teacher would make sure Mum became a widow? She'd be wrecked, and he couldn't do that to her—Dad was her soul mate, and to be parted from him would mean she wouldn't want to live anymore. That she wouldn't stick around for Shaq was something he'd always sensed, that her love for Dad was so much greater.

Maybe that's why the teacher had been able to convince him to hate her so easily.

Like he'd thought earlier, clarity had seeped in, he saw things so differently now, ashamed of what he'd let himself believe, how he'd acted on it. Dayton had had the privilege of being at home inside his skin, something that had been taken away from Shaq. He'd envied him, the jealousy so intense it had ended up with him sinking that knife into him again and again, the rage directed at the teacher, not the poor bastard on the ground a few steps away from the bus stop.

Shaq was glad those lads had got up and held him until the police arrived. It was the only way to stop him, being arrested and sent down. In here, he wouldn't kill Anaisha. She was happy in her skin, too, and she wouldn't have been safe with him around. Maybe that's why he'd chosen that night, that moment to kill her brother, because he'd known those lads were there. Maybe the good part of him that had shown its face again lately, had whispered that his warped thinking had to end.

He maintained to anyone who asked that he didn't feel bad, worried word would get back to the teacher if he admitted he hated himself for what he'd done and said. It was like he'd been a different person, and the one he was learning all about now was who he must have been before the teacher had whispered in his ear. Who he was supposed to be.

Once the teacher was dead, Shaq would speak out.

Until then, he'd keep the secret.

Keep his parents safe.

Chapter Nine

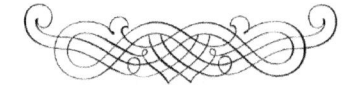

The next morning had dawned bright, the sky cluttered with white cotton-ball clouds. Anaisha should feel all of the joys of spring like her colleagues seemed to; it was amazing what a dash of sunshine did to the spirit. But the weather wasn't exactly on her radar. She had other things to think about, like keeping a secret from everyone for some time now, even though she knew damn well help was out there. *And* she should know better than to stay where she wasn't safe anymore. But knowing how to advise the public in these matters was vastly different to when you were going through it yourself. At work, no emotions were involved apart from the expected empathy extended towards those in a DV relationship. In her reality, *all* of her emotions were a tangled mess whenever Ben decided to get arsey.

She'd only been living with him for a year, seeing him for two altogether. He was a copper, too, an older-than-her detective at another station. Held in high regard, someone people looked up to, one of the reasons she'd agreed to go out on a date with him. Bloody hell, if only she hadn't been so desperate to take her mind off Dayton's death and her parents' grief, she'd never have fallen for his charm. She wouldn't have needed him as a distraction.

Pressure at work meant he was moody most of the time at home lately, which was his excuse for how he now behaved towards her. She had no idea what case he worked on, yet previously, he'd been more than happy to open up to her. It must be something sensitive if he couldn't share the details; sometimes they were sworn to secrecy, warned not to discuss anything with their other halves, but she was a police officer and would be speaking to *another* police officer, so surely it would be okay. Whenever she tried to talk about Operation Balustrade, needing to vent, he cut her off, saying he had enough work of his own filling his mind. He was definitely a bear with a sore head.

Except last night it had been more than that, just like it had been more than that on a smattering of nights previously. He'd hit her, a backhanded slap across the face. For a second he'd been stunned at his anger, as he had before, which didn't make sense. If he'd chosen to hit her, why appear surprised when he had? Why was shock written all over him? But then he'd blamed her, saying if she hadn't pushed and prodded at him to open up, he wouldn't have walloped her. If there was no extra pressure coming from her, he wouldn't have felt the need to strike out. He was a good at that, gaslighting, laying the blame at her door, and while she knew it was happening, it was as if it wasn't in a way—or maybe she was trying to convince herself it couldn't possibly be happening to *her*, a copper who knew what this behaviour could lead to.

What it *had* led to.

Even her being the victim of coercive control and manipulation was enough reason to leave him, but—and perhaps pathetically, some would say—she kept recalling what he was like before the pressure had come in. But the rational side of her said no matter how stressed he was, he shouldn't be treating her this way—and she shouldn't be accepting of it.

It was up to her to stop this.

Fuck's sake.

Thankfully, the frozen bag of peas against her face had taken away the swelling, and she'd put concealer and foundation on to cover the little bruise on her cheekbone. She'd sat up contemplating her future long after he'd stormed out. Only his name was on the tenancy agreement and utility bills, so she had no worries there—and even if hers was, she'd soon get them taken off. All she had to do was pack a couple of suitcases, her clothes and a few ornaments her only possessions. She'd left a lot at home with Mum and Dad, putting it in boxes and storing it in the loft alongside Dayton's things, which Mum had finally let go of, clearing his bedroom out so she could use it as an office.

Dad wasn't best pleased. He'd wanted to keep Dayton's room as a shrine.

Yes, Anaisha was going to do it. Get away. Leave Ben and his nasty fists, his slaps. Whether she'd get him in the shit for hitting her was another matter. She *should* do it, but his warning that no one would believe her wouldn't go away. Annoyed she'd let him worm his way into her head, she gritted her teeth.

No more excuses. She'd sort a flat out for herself tomorrow, her day off. But then she remembered she'd booked a visit to see Shaq in the morning.

Panic crept in, the kind where she spun too many plates, had too much to deal with at once, and she took deep breaths to calm her racing heart. Stared at her monitor on the desk at the station.

Concentrate on that. One thing at a time.

Amateur had yet to log on, and it was doing a number on her nerves, adding fuel to the fire regarding Ben. Why wasn't Amateur chatting already like he usually did? What if he didn't turn up later? What if her mentioning the reverse

Google search had frightened him off? She should never have suggested mentioning it to him. Oliver should never have agreed. What the hell had they been thinking? It was already twelve o'clock, and the team had to get going soon in order to stand in place, and with no contact, Operation Balustrade might well go to shit.

Oliver walked in and clapped to get everyone's attention. "Right, here's the order of play."

He went through the details, bringing up Google Street View of the area outside the Odeon so they all knew where they were going to stand. Nearby, a Costa would give two officers a chance to sit outside and pretend they were a couple on a date. Anaisha would sit outside Pizza Express on the wall there, watching the proceedings, while Oliver and Fay, his DS, would stand closer to the Odeon. One other officer would hang around outside McDonald's, the other by the fountain in the middle of the courtyard area.

Briefing over, they all filed out of the station, Anaisha minus the red jacket she'd told Amateur she'd put on. Sunglasses covered her distinctive eyes, a baseball cap pulled low, her hair stuffed into it. She'd taken into account what Flint had said about the pervert recognising her, although Oliver had also told her to disguise herself earlier.

They split into two unmarked cars, Anaisha in the back of one with Fay, and the journey seemed to take forever. Her stomach kept going over, and her chest tightened every time she thought about scanning the crowd and Amateur recognising her mouth from the photos she'd sent him.

In a nearby car park, they went their separate ways, Anaisha finding her spot on the wall and settling onto it. The sun shone, although the air was a bit nippy. She shoved her hands in her coat pockets and studied people one by one. A few kids stood or sat around on stone benches, sipping from McDonald's cups and eating burgers, but no lads were alone, and surprisingly, no child wore red. She glanced over at the officer couple drinking their coffees and spotted two men sitting alone. One, clean-shaven with a shock of ginger hair, read his phone, and the other with a beard and sunglasses people-watched.

Or was he waiting for her to turn up?

She quickly averted her gaze, taking her phone out to get hold of Oliver. Yes, another colleague may well have spotted Mr Beard, but it didn't hurt to make sure. Once she'd sent the warning, she clicked the London Teens app and checked her message box. Amateur had responded to her earlier comment where she'd asked if they were still meeting today. She didn't have any alert tones on, but the time beneath the message stated it had arrived one minute ago. Could it have been sent by the man she'd just seen on his phone, the clean-shaven one? Or had Mr Beard sent it after she'd looked away?

Another man entered the equation. Jeans, black puffa jacket, trainers, and a navy-blue baseball cap, sunglasses. Fucking hell, was that *Flint*? She shook her head at herself. Of course it wouldn't be him. He just had a similar nose, that was all, and besides, Flint hadn't had longish stubble yesterday when she'd spoken to him, and he certainly wasn't tanned. He leaned on the wall beside the Odeon doors and took a phone out, holding it up. Maybe he was taking pictures to put on Facebook or Instagram.

She brought her screen back to life, alarmed she'd received another message.

AMATEUR_PHOTOGRAPHER: WHERE ARE YOU? I CAN'T SEE YOU ANYWHERE.

She couldn't reply yet. If he was watching, he'd be looking for anyone answering. Instead, she informed Oliver that Amateur had made contact and she was going inside the toilets in Costa so she could respond without him seeing her. The team could then try to pick up on a man or boy replying to her.

A thumbs-up emoji arrived, so she got up and casually walked into the coffee shop. In the loo, she locked the door and sat on the closed toilet seat for a moment in case their target had seen her getting up. She composed another message to Oliver to ensure her planned response was going to be okay. He replied that it was and he'd alert the other officers, but Anaisha was to stay put.

Loves_Risqué_Shots: Sorry, I'm in McDonald's. Needed some lunch. Come and find me.

Amateur_Photographer: Okay.

She'd stay here until she got word from Oliver.

Chapter Ten

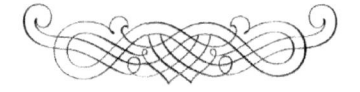

Amateur sat outside Costa nursing his latte. He wished he'd found out where Risqué lived ages ago so he could have got this job done and dusted already. She hadn't given up her address, though, and he hadn't pressed for it a second time—that would have looked weird and might have sent her running. He could say it didn't matter now because Risqué had asked to meet him, but something was off. He sensed it in the air, and that fucking bloke leaning on the Odeon wall kept staring his way, or maybe that was Amateur's overactive imagination.

He'd clocked each and every one of the people around him since he'd arrived at midday, wanting to get here earlier so he could settle his nerves, take stock. The three coffees he'd eked out over the past hour and a half wreaked havoc on his bladder, but nipping to the toilet wasn't an option. The appointed time had come, and if he got up to use the loo now, he might miss her altogether.

She'd worried him by saying she'd done a reverse Google search on his picture. He'd got away with using the same one since the start of this little venture years ago, and no other girls had been clever enough to check it. This child was savvy and might become a bit of a problem—he usually steered clear of those with intelligence, but as she hadn't displayed much of it during their chats, up until she'd mentioned what she'd done, he'd thought he was safe to continue with her.

Now, he had second thoughts. Maybe he ought to close down his username, find another girl. But his current customer liked how she looked. After several tries at snagging the right type of girl for Client 10—some of them didn't have selfies as profile pictures, so he hadn't been able to see them straight off the bat—Amateur had come up trumps when she'd sent him her picture. 10 had put in a request for black and white ethnic heritage last year, prepared to wait patiently, and yesterday Amateur had been able to tell him she'd be on her way soon, that he'd come to the point where he could take her.

He wasn't stupid enough to nab her here—too many people and cameras—and while he'd grown a beard in readiness for the day he took her, one he'd shave after the snatch, he still preferred to be careful.

Just like all the others, one child per year, he'd take her from her home or, if she was out in the dark, he'd pick her up then, but only from a place where he wouldn't be seen. The payment for girls was a million, and he also charged hefty expenses which he lived off as his wages, not to mention the interest. After all, it was him taking the risks while the clients sat back and waited for the goods to be delivered. She was his last kidnap, then he could mosey off into the sunset and live a full and rich life abroad, leaving his wife and child behind. They were a bind anyway, both of them got on his nerves, and he should never have got married. He spent half his time trying to teach her how to behave, and it was draining him.

Ten million was a lot to live off, and he had a decade of his life to make up for, years he'd lost in limbo, building up his fortune. So many hours spent in front of a computer in his garage, pretending to be a sixteen-year-old boy. Years spent living with a woman he'd quickly grown to hate, a child he disliked. He only kept them around so he could fuck with the wife's head.

Each time a girl had gone missing, the police professed to be doing their best to bring them home, but of course, none of them had been reunited with their parents while alive. Some of their bodies, however, had turned up later down the line, discarded and no longer of any use. Other bodies had been hidden, perhaps buried, never to be found, but the latest three snatches were still with their buyers. Did he feel bad that he stole girls only for them to be killed once they'd started to mature? Nah. Money was king. His life was all about the readies.

This was his first girl from London Teens. VPNs were marvellous things, as he'd discovered on the other social media sites he'd used, and after one of his grab-the-goods events, he always ditched his computer and bought another one. Started fresh. New VPN access point, new site, the lot.

A few months ago, London Teens had been closed pending an investigation, and he'd thought his time there was up, that he'd have to go elsewhere to groom and lure, but it had popped back up again. He'd sighed with relief, because he'd already put in a lot of groundwork, getting his username seen in the forums as someone who could be trusted. The resulting news coverage of Summer Meeks' death was a pest, though fortunately, it hadn't stopped Risqué from engaging with him. Maybe that's why she'd done the reverse Google, attempting to keep herself safe.

Why wait until today to mention it, though? Why carry on speaking to him if she knew he wasn't who he'd said he was? Was that something he should be worried about? Should he look into whether people had to be eighteen and over to upload images to the stock sites? Would she have gone that far in her snooping? If she had, she'd have seen that image was uploaded years ago, so surely she would've mentioned it before the cinema date.

That was another reason things were off.

Fuck it, he shouldn't have come today.

He opened the chat box on his phone to talk to her again then changed his mind. Let her stew in McDonald's then come out to try and find him. Bloody hell, what was keeping her? He'd hoped to follow her home. Take her from her bed tonight. Contrary to what some people might think, he hated that bit. Didn't get off on it at all. The only part that floated his boat was seeing a new money dump in his bank. The girls were a means to an end. All they represented were pound signs.

He gave in, ignoring his gut instinct, and made contact.

AMATEUR_PHOTOGRAPHER: CAN'T SEE YOU. WILL WAIT OUTSIDE.

LOVES_RISQUÉ_SHOTS: [HEART EMOJI]

AMATEUR_PHOTOGRAPHER: [HEART EMOJI X3]

He closed the chat box. Accessed a text sent from one of his mates. God, he really didn't need this shit right now. He looked forward to the moment when his other troubles were over. When he didn't have to deal with this—crap involving his wife.

You should have left her, then. Paid her off in a divorce. It's not like you don't have the money.

EVAN: SHE STILL HASN'T COME BACK TO THE BAR. SHE WENT OFF TO SIGN SOME PAPERS.

Amateur switched into his other self, Kendall, and gritted his teeth. Ivory was doing his fucking nut in. He'd told her she needed another job, that he couldn't carry them all on his wages as a brickie—a trade he'd never engaged in. She had no idea about the millions in his bank; he had to keep things authentic, make out he was a regular bloke. His secret profession had to remain on the quiet for obvious reasons. He'd only married her as a cover, to build a life where no one would suspect what he did and who he really was. Something he regretted. He should have just been a player, shagging as many women as he could, like with Marnie.

Frustration bubbling over at his two lives colliding, he glanced across at McDonald's.

No girl in a red jacket.

He swung his attention to the man leaning on the Odeon wall.

No, something *definitely* wasn't right. Why the hell was the cunt staring at him like that? The man lifted his sunglasses and made eye contact, quickly lowering them again. Jerked his head for Kendall to follow him. What was that all about?

What if he was a copper? And if not, what the chuff did he want?

Why single me out?

Shit, is it the client?

Kendall checked his surroundings. No one else appeared suss, but in the absence of Risqué and his instincts screaming at him to get out of there, he rose, walking in the opposite direction to the man. He took his phone out to message the girl who could ruin everything but paused. He'd wait for a bit in case he was being watched by others. If they saw him use his phone, then she picked hers up…

Two minutes of strolling towards the car park, and he tapped his screen.

AMATEUR_PHOTOGRAPHER: I'M LEAVING. I THINK YOU'RE MESSING ME ABOUT.

Loves_Risqué_Shots: LOL. I just thought the same about you. There's no one here with a Man Utd shirt on.

Amateur_Photographer: We'll arrange another date or something. I'm too pissed off now.

Loves_Risqué_Shots: I'm sorry. There's just so many people here, and I couldn't find you anywhere.

Kendall didn't respond. He needed to get to his garage and regroup. The sensation of impending danger wouldn't go away, so maybe it was best he contacted the client to say the deal was off. He had plenty of money now, adding a tenth million was just being greedy, so all that was left to do was book a flight. He already had his getaway suitcase and passport at the garage.

He got into his Kia and sent a message to 10.

K: Problem. Were you at the Odeon just now?

Client 10: No. We agreed I wouldn't attend for the final sign-off on the girl.

K: Did you send someone else?

Client 10: No.

K: She wasn't there yet claimed she was. Aborting mission.

Client 10: For now or for good?

K: For good. Too risky.

Client 10: I want those expenses back if the goods aren't forthcoming.

K: Sending them in a sec.

While that was a fucking cheek, he'd earned those expenses, he couldn't be arsed to argue. He sent them then gunned the engine. "Fuck this for a game of soldiers, I'm off."

***

He'd transformed the garage he'd bought, one in a long row, by covering the breeze-block walls with boards, plaster, and a coat of black paint. Laminate flooring in a nice dark grey. He'd removed the up-and-over door and had the front bricked up, leaving enough space for a normal door. It resembled a man cave, and he'd spent many a year in here, chasing the girls, chasing the readies. A black leather sofa bed sat down the right-hand side, an oak coffee table on a silver rug in front of it. His desk, at the back, top left, housed a high-spec gaming computer which he played on in between messaging girls. Next to it, a row of two kitchen cabinets, a toaster, kettle, and microwave on top. Oh, and his washing-up bowl, something he pissed in when he couldn't be bothered to go outside and have a slash up against a tree.

He was going to miss this, being lord of his tiny manor.

But he wouldn't miss Ivory. Even though he loved doing it, fucking with her head had got old recently, as had punching her to vent his frustrations. As for sex, he'd avoided that, choosing to dabble with Marnie instead. He needed a new outlet, a new woman, maybe several. As for Remy, he was a whiny little bastard. Kendall had never bonded with him, hadn't even *wanted* kids, and while he regularly told Ivory he'd kidnap him, that was nothing but a threat.

The only reason he'd kept the pair of them around was for the air of respectability they provided. He'd enjoyed exerting control over her, forcing her to do whatever he wanted, but yeah, it had worn thin.

He sat at the desk and booted up his computer, finding a cheap flight. One was leaving in five hours, so he'd hang about here for a while, get Uber Eats to deliver his dinner, something he did on the regular. He liked the idea of Ivory cooking him food and it going to waste, him blaming her for it. Gaslighting and its results, her face crumpling with confusion, had become a hobby.

He booked his ticket to Alicante and sent his computer on the road back to factory settings. He'd take the car home. Ivory could have it, a parting gift. Then he'd walk to the Dog and Bone, dump the hard drive in a public bin, and get a taxi to the airport. The house was rented, so when she realised he wasn't coming home, she'd have to sort things with the landlord. By that time, he'd be sunning himself beside the pool at a hotel where he'd stay until he could buy a villa, no fucks given.

He ordered a McDonald's—Risqué had put it into his bloody head, hadn't she—and sat on the sofa to wait, picking up his phone and removing the London Teens app and various others. Tinder. Fitness 101. Spyware linked to Ivory's phone—he'd been tempted to see where she was one last time but actually didn't give a toss. He intended to ditch this mobile, but the act of deleting everything gave him a sense of power during a time when he'd lost control, which didn't happen often. Risqué had called the shots today, not him, and she'd saved herself without even realising it. Unless 10 jumped onto London Teens himself and started chatting to her, she was safe from kidnap and incarceration. She'd never know how close she'd come to living in a cellar or attic room until she'd grown too old—sixteen was the limit for most clients to keep their purchases—her body discarded once it was of no use.

A tap on the door signalled his dinner had arrived quickly; it did sometimes, seeing as McDonald's wasn't that far away. He chucked his phone on the sofa and got up. He'd already tipped the driver via the app so opened the door, his hand out ready to take the bag.

The man from the cinema stared at him through sunglasses that reflected Kendall's shocked expression back at him.

Fuck.

He went to slam the door, but the bloke stuck his foot out.

"I don't think so." He held up some ID. *Police* ID. John Stokes, a detective inspector.

I bloody knew it.

Kendall's arsehole spasmed, his heart beating too fast, and he held his palms up. There was absolutely no proof of what he'd done bar the clients' names still in his phone. Why hadn't they been the first thing he'd got rid of?

Of all the stupid things I've done…

He'd have to wing it. "Look, I don't know why you're here, but I've done nothing wrong."

"Who were you waiting for outside Costa?"

"No one!"

"You'd better tell me, otherwise I'm likely to get nasty."

Kendall sighed "A girlfriend, all right? I met her on a dating app. We were meant to go to the cinema, but she didn't turn up. Where's the crime in that?"

"London Teens?"

Kendall worked hard to compose his face into an expression of puzzlement. Had the police been watching him online all this time? Was that why the site had been closed because spyware or something had been installed on it? "I don't know what you're talking about, mate."

"Oh, I think you do. I'm almost sure your username's Amateur_Photographer, but clearly you're not sixteen."

Jesus Christ… "What?"

"And she's called Loves_Risqué_Shots, and she isn't thirteen. She's a police officer in her twenties."

Kendall wasn't sure how to react without giving himself away. He'd been speaking to her for months, and she was a *copper*?

Fuck me, she's good at her job. I had no sodding clue. Come on, think. Get yourself out of this bastard mess. "You're off your rocker, you are."

John pushed Kendall back. He stumbled, and the bloke came in and shut the door.

John stared at the computer screen. "Factory reset by any chance? Someone's got something to hide. You know, it's so obvious, what and who you are. It stood out that you were trying to act casual today, when really, you were on edge. I'm right, aren't I?"

"John, please…"

"That's not my real name. I'm Bryan Flint, and yes, I am a police officer, but I also happen to work for The Brothers. I'm sure you've heard of them. Now sit your arse down. I'm going to let them know what I suspect, and as you won't admit it to me, I can sure as shit guarantee you'll admit it to them. They have ways and means of making people talk…"

Shaking, Kendall lowered himself to the sofa, reaching across for his phone. If he could get a message to Evan…

"Throw that on the floor," Flint ordered.

Reluctantly, Kendall tossed onto the rug, his mind scrabbling to find a way to help himself here. *Calm down*. It was okay, the Uber driver would be here soon. Whoever it was would help if Kendall called out to him.

Unless Flint tells them he's a copper…

Kendall closed his eyes. He was so fucked.

Chapter Eleven

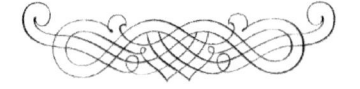

Flint breathed a sigh of relief. He'd recognised Amateur as a fellow pervert a mile away — which was disturbing, considering Flint was one. Did people sense it in him, too? Did he think he was gadding about undetected when other people knew damn well what went on inside his head? Add to that the computer being reset and this garage being a posh little hideaway, and he had his ticket out of a sticky situation. It was so obvious this lair was used for nefarious things because of it being a garage, not a house or flat. Flint was almost jealous of the setup. It could be a bachelor pad.

Was this man a bachelor? Did he live here? If so, where did he shower? There wasn't even a sink, just a plastic bowl on a kitchen unit beside a toaster, kettle, and microwave. Large flagons of water stood on the floor, likely used for washing up. Maybe he drove to petrol stations, ones with showers in them for lorry drivers.

Nah, this was a bolthole. Somewhere to hide while being a perv. He probably lived a respectable life somewhere beside his respectable wife and children. Even a respectable dog.

Flint snapped his mind back to the reason he'd found himself here. The fact he'd been Fishy_For_Life had played on his mind something chronic ever since he'd heard Summer was dead, but now he had someone to blame it on. An answer to his prayers. Yes, it was a lie, Amateur might not have spoken to Summer at all, but if the twins could just get him to admit to chatting to Anaisha, then the rest would fall into place. Flint planned to say the bloke wouldn't confess to Summer because she'd snuffed it, but look, they had their man, and justice could be served.

Getting away with what he'd done brought on a smile.

"What are you smirking at?" Amateur sniped.

"None of your business." Except it was, considering Flint was using him as a scapegoat. Still, he wouldn't tell him that.

Keeping the man in his peripheral, he glanced around for something to tie him up with. There wasn't much, so he'd have to improvise. He ordered Amateur to collect what he needed, watching him the whole time, waiting for him to spring towards him, try to take him down. The fella was nervous but obeyed, maybe hoping if he complied he'd be set free eventually. He'd used a VPN, for fuck's sake, so there was no proof he'd even done anything, nothing Flint could show the twins to prove this was who they'd been looking for. He'd have to play this carefully.

Amateur brought the items to the sofa and sat. "I'm doing this to show I'm innocent. I don't have the foggiest what you're on about, so you tie me up or whatever if it makes you feel better."

"Like you don't have the foggiest regarding Summer Meeks? Her face has been all over the news, so you can't tell me you haven't seen her. Or maybe you know her as Mermaid."

"What?"

"She killed herself because of you." *Because of me.*

"I don't even know her!"

"That's what I'd say if I'd been caught waiting to meet a minor. Your sort make me sick." Your sort. *My sort.* Christ, Flint really ought to stick to turning over a new leaf. He had the perfect out here, a way to completely wipe the slate clean. If he could just control his urges to do the envelope thing, everything would be all right.

He got on with tying Amateur's wrists and ankles. The flexes he used weren't that long, he could only wrap them round once, but they'd do.

"I'll phone the twins in a minute, then we can really get this show on the road."

A tap at the door startled him, and his stomach rolled over. Had one of Anaisha's team spotted him and followed him here? How the hell was he going to get himself out of being at the cinema and not phoning it in that he'd followed a suspect? Not to mention Anaisha possibly getting into trouble for telling him aspects of Operation Balustrade.

"Are you expecting anyone?" he asked.

Amateur didn't respond.

Flint went over and looked through the peephole. A man in a helmet stood there, the visor up. A spotty kid, maybe eighteen or nineteen. Flint twisted the lock, took the proffered bag, and slammed the door shut just as Amateur shouted, "Wait!"

Flint turned to him. "Nice try." He put the bag and cup on the desk and took his phone out. He didn't message the twins straight away, he'd toy with this prick first. It felt good, having this much influence over someone else's feelings, just like it had when he'd coerced girls to leave those envelopes.

This could be the outlet he'd been searching for, a way to exert control.

Maybe he'd get used to being The Brothers' bitch after all.

Chapter Twelve

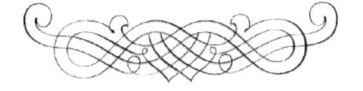

Anaisha had joined the police. Working on response shit her up more often than not. She faced some of the worst in society, and she'd bet half of them carried knives. One wrong word from her, and they could whip one out and stab her. She lived in daily fear that she'd die on the pavement like her brother, that her parents would have to suffer all over again.

Guilt poked her regularly for choosing this career, Mum and Dad worrying day after day that their youngest child would die, too. But Anaisha couldn't shift that need she had to get some form of justice for others so they didn't have to suffer as much. The only justice she'd had was Shaq being in prison, but that was no justice at all. He wasn't dead, and until he was, the right punishment hadn't been meted out.

Maybe she'd secretly hoped that by being a copper she'd get to know the type of people who'd arrange a hit on Shaq. Someone, somewhere, had connections with people in that prison, and if she knew who they were and had the money, she'd pay them to get rid of him. But she'd have to be careful. Her going around asking questions would be noted, and she couldn't let the finger of blame point at her if Shaq died.

Not if, when.

How it would go down, she didn't know, but deep in her soul she knew he'd die before he reached thirty. She'd given herself that goal, enough years to pass where Anaisha and her parents wouldn't be accused of setting his murder up. Mind you, she was aware of how things worked now, so of course they'd be suspects.

So she didn't get coiled up, she concentrated on her surroundings. PC Lee Potts sat in the driver's seat, cruising around the East End, the pair of them on the lookout for anyone who appeared suss. This was the way most of their days went unless a call came in for them to respond to. Already this morning they'd attended a fatality in the home, an old man dying and only being discovered when the smell alerted his next-door neighbour. Then there was the woman who'd been wandering the streets in her underwear, and the lad who'd been shoplifting.

Anaisha frowned. The driver ahead acted oddly, swerving. She'd soon learned how to spot when someone wasn't on the level, and with no reason for the car to slew towards the middle line, she nudged Lee.

"What's he doing, weaving like that?" She pointed at the windscreen.

"Fuck's sake."

Lee put the lights on, a quick blip of the siren alerting the driver that he was being followed. The car pulled over, Lee drawing up behind him, and they got out to deal with him. He tried to get out of his vehicle without giving it away that he was drunk, which was highly evident, plus he stank of booze. Anaisha recognised him, and her stomach lurched. She gave Lee a look that told him he'd be better off dealing with this and she'd explain why later.

Lee asked him to walk to the pavement, and they observed how the bloke stumbled.

"I'm sorry," the man said. "I shouldn't have got behind the wheel. I didn't mean—"

"Name, please," Lee asked.

"Donny Yarsly."

Shaq's father; she'd seen him in court on the day of sentencing, although his mother hadn't been there— Mum had sympathy for her regarding that, but Dad was angry that the woman hadn't had the decency to face them. Anaisha had never seen the woman before so wouldn't know her anyway. She'd heard Donny had turned to the bottle for comfort. Some said the shame of his son being a killer had sent him into the arms of vodka pretty early on. Shaq's mother had become a recluse, only leaving the house to visit him.

Lee glanced at Anaisha, and she returned to the car for a breathalyser kit. While Lee tested Donny, she studied the poor man. He looked much older since she'd last seen him. Haggard, as if all the happiness had been drained out of him. Much like her father. Two men who'd lost their sons forever but in different ways. But at least Donny still got to see his if he chose to. He could speak to him. All Dad had was a gravestone that didn't answer whenever he sat on the ground beside it and chatted to his boy.

All this, the aftermath, could have been avoided if Donny and his wife had paid more attention to the changes in their son and tried to do something about whatever the hell had gone on inside his head. She hated to blame this broken fella who'd just failed the breathalyser test spectacularly, but he had to take some responsibility for how his child had turned out.

For a few seconds, she hated him as much as she hated Shaq. Then she snapped into work mode and got on with the job in hand. By the time they'd arranged for Donny's car to be towed, taken him to the station, and were back out on the road again, sorting out an argument between a shop owner and a customer, she had no time to think about the impact Shaq had on his parents—and on hers. For the rest of the day she purposely shut any bad thoughts out regarding her personal issues and focused on the present, what was right in front of her.

Her shift came to an end, and she went home, exhausted. Mum had her bright face on this evening, the mask she wore when she didn't want grief to take the upper hand in front of Anaisha. It was a hard taskmaster, that grief—Anaisha should know, it flogged her on the daily.

"Thank God you're back," Mum said.

And it was obvious, her relief, how she'd been worrying all day that her daughter wouldn't come home and there'd be another knock on the door, two more officers in uniform there to tell her Anaisha had died in the line of duty. Anaisha felt guilty about her choice of profession sometimes, but like Janine had said, she shouldn't put her life on hold just because what she did every day upset them. That was their cross to bear, not hers.

"Of course I am." Anaisha sat at the table, her body aching. "Did you have a good day?"

"As good as it can be. You know."

Yes, she knew. As good as it could be without Dayton's laughter, his presence, his caring nature. "I saw his dad today."

"Oh."

"Driving while drunk."

"Ah... The poor man."

"I know, but he brought Shaq up, remember."

"True, but some children, no matter what you do, turn out wrong. You could bring two kids up the exact same way and one could be bad to the bone."

Anaisha couldn't argue with that. Dayton had been pure and good, but a percentage of her was bad. Then again, she'd still be fully good if her brother wasn't dead. She wouldn't have entertained Shaq dying a slow, painful death or being killed in prison if he hadn't become obsessed with Dayton and stabbed him.

Life's choices had a way of changing you forever, and the fact it was someone else's *choice, something out of her control, rankled. She'd been changed forever by his actions, as had Mum and Dad, and Shaq's parents, maybe even Shaq himself.*

It was unfair.

"Fancy a takeaway?" Anaisha asked. "My treat."

"I was just going to start dinner."

"But you look tired."

Mum nodded and sank onto a chair. "All right, you've twisted my arm."

And there it was, proof of how easy it could be to influence another person, bend them to your will. How, if you chose someone who was weak and had no energy or courage to fight back, you could manipulate their decisions. More and more lately, Anaisha was convinced that was what had happened to Shaq. From the little snippets he gave her regarding the 'damage' he kept mentioning, she had a feeling he was trying to tell her something but felt he couldn't.

She'd get to the bottom of it one day.

Mum rose again. "Let me just call your dad down so he can choose what he wants. He's had a bad day and went up for a little nap after he got back from work."

Anaisha understood. Sleep made you forget if you were lucky enough to be gifted with a dreamless break from reality—unless your worries seeped out and formed pictures and sounds and words that coalesced into a nightmare that ended up chasing you awake. Many a time she'd followed Dayton past that bus stop like a ghost, blocking Shaq's path so he couldn't get to him, but he walked straight through her and killed Dayton anyway. Sometimes the scenario changed if Anaisha gained control of the dream. Then she stalked Shaq, and together, she and Dayton murdered him instead.

Mum left the room, and Anaisha stuck the kettle on. She didn't care what Dad chose to eat. All she wanted was for Mum to not have to cook and for them to sit around the table and try to have a nice family dinner. She usually started off talking about Dayton, wanting them to remember the fun times, but it was still too painful for her parents. They couldn't seem to see past the murder and that he wasn't with them anymore. They fixated on it, but wasn't it healthier to embrace the life he'd led and be grateful he'd been there at all rather than wallow that he wasn't?

Dad shuffled in, his scowl in place. It was a permanent resident on his face now, the way he looked all the time. He didn't smile or laugh anymore, as though if he did, that would be wrong. That to find joy in life when his son was dead wasn't allowed. She wished she could help them to move on from the point they were stuck in, but a counsellor at work had told her that everyone coped differently and it wasn't her place to impose her way of mourning on them.

Just like it wasn't their place to impose theirs on her.

Sometimes, she wished Dad would be grateful she was still alive, *she still needed him.*

"What do you fancy?" she asked him.

"Doesn't matter to me."

Nothing ever did. He sat and stared at the bowl of fruit on the table, fruit that would have been eaten by now if Dayton were here. Mum bought it out of habit, and every time it ended up in the bin, the skin wrinkled.

Mum glanced at Anaisha—leave him be*—and Anaisha turned to make the tea. She handed the cups out, then sat and brought up her contact list.*

"Chinese?" she suggested to Mum.

"That'd be nice."

"The usual?"

"Yes, the usual."

And so it was, this life, everything exactly the same but so different. Anaisha phoned the local takeaway and gave her order, asking for the cash-on-delivery option. Then they sat and drank their tea in silence, and she'd bet her parents were thinking the same as her.

That the table was empty without Dayton sitting at it.

Chapter Thirteen

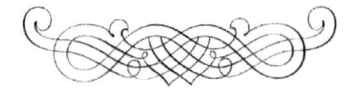

Marnie Fields hadn't liked being told to keep away from Kendall Reynolds at first, but George reckoned she'd got the gist about the bastard's behaviour now. They'd paid her a visit at her scummy house, the smell a tad rancid, as if she hadn't emptied the kitchen bin for weeks. She'd let them in thinking she was going to bag herself a nice little earner, saying she'd love to be a grass and she could do with the money. George had soon disabused her of that notion over a weak-as-piss instant coffee that he refused to finish drinking. Mind you, she was unemployed and had a lot of time on her hands, so maybe she *could* be an informant. He'd explained what Ivory and Remy had been through, and the woman seemed suitably shocked about it.

George stood in the dining side of her small kitchen.

Jesus, that washing up will be walking out of here in a minute. It's that mouldy it's got legs. Maybe she's struggling with depression.

He thought about sending a cleaning crew round to smarten the place up. Some people would take offence at that, so he'd gauge which type Marnie was before he offered. For all he knew, she might welcome the help.

"When did you start seeing Kendall?" he asked.

She shrugged. "A few weeks ago. I've never really got on with Ivory, she acts like she's up her own arse most of the time, so I got pleasure out of doing it with him behind her back."

They'd learned a lot from Sharon at Haven, about how some women behaved while in a DV relationship, and George was just about to give Marnie some true facts regarding that when Greg butted in.

"The only reason she'd have acted like that was because it was safer." Greg gave her a filthy look. "Abused people have to be so careful. Some of them can't make friends because their partners say they're not allowed, they want to isolate them, and in Ivory's situation, she was too scared in case she let the secrets slip."

Marnie's eyebrows bunched. "What secrets?"

George sighed. "You don't get it, do you? The secrets in her *marriage*. The abuse."

"Oh, right. Poor cow. I feel sorry for her now." She frowned. "But that doesn't make sense. We had a barney earlier, right, and she told me if she caught me even breathing near Kendall she'd have me. Why say that if she wasn't happy with him?"

"To maintain the charade," George said. "I take it you've never suffered domestic violence. If you had, you'd understand."

"Can't say I have. I tend to stick up for myself, and men know that. Where is she now?"

"I can't tell you that, but she's safe. *Don't* tell Kendall she's not at home."

"Fine. Not being funny, but what has all this got to do with me? I mean, yeah, I shagged her husband a few times, but it's not like I want to set up home with him or anything. I'm not a homewrecker."

"Good, because we came to warn you that if you continue seeing him, you could end up like Ivory. We're trying to prevent the shit flying before it gets anywhere near the fan. When are you next due to see him?"

"We don't text or anything like that, there's no dates set. It's just if we see each other in the pub or something and the fancy takes us. I won't be going anywhere near him now, I can tell you."

"What's your mental health like?" George asked.

She squirmed. Hid her possible embarrassment by barking, "You what?"

"This place is a tip. Is that because you're a lazy cow or have you lost the will to keep it clean and tidy?"

"What do you want to know for?"

"Because despite you fucking about with Kendall, you're our resident, and if you're in a bind, we'd like to help."

"In what way?"

"By sending someone round here to scrub this place for a start."

Her shoulders relaxed, and she showed them a little of her vulnerability. "Things are tough. I'm skint. Can't seem to get my act together. I've got no oomph to get the hoover out."

"Then two women will be round later. They'll sort your house out, get your washing down Lil's. You said you'd love to be a grass." George noted the expected reaction—her eyes lighting up and a sly smile appearing. "If you ring us as soon as Kendall comes home, there's a grand in it for you." He tossed her a business card with their work burner number on it.

"I'd have to sit by the window to know when he's back."

"Then that's what you'll do."

"But he sometimes doesn't come home. He stays overnight somewhere."

"So we've heard."

"I could be sitting there for *hours*."

"For a grand, it's worth it, isn't it?"

"Suppose so." Said like that much money was nothing to her, when it was probably everything she needed to get herself out of a financial hole.

"Give me your number."

She recited it, and Greg plugged it into their phone, which then bleeped. He checked the message and raised his eyebrows, turning the screen round so only George could see it.

Flint: Think I've got the geezer who was involved with Summer Meeks. Explain later, but I'm at his garage. I've told him you'll be dropping by. Will you?

George nodded at Greg for him to respond that yes, they would be bloody dropping by. "We have to go, Marnie. Thanks for the coffee."

"You didn't even drink it."

"Because it tasted like shit. Don't forget, as soon as he's back, tell us, and keep this to yourself else there'll be trouble."

"I'm not stupid."

"That's debateable, considering you went with a married man." George walked out and sat in the passenger seat of the van. Once Greg had got in, he asked, "Where's this garage?"

"There's a row of them down Barton Way. Flint said it's kitted out nice, so that doesn't gel with Ivory saying he hasn't got much money." Greg drove off, clipping his seat belt one-handed.

"He probably got it all on tick. I bet it's where he does the dirty deed, talking to those girls. I wonder how Flint caught up with him?"

"Fuck knows, but we'll soon find out."

George took a mini bag of Tangfastics out of the glove box. "We'll need to get grub at some point. I'm fucking starving."

"Your stomach rules you."

George had emptied the bag by the time they'd drawn up outside the garages situated behind a line of houses. A Kia and Flint's car sat outside.

"There it is," Greg said. "The one with the normal door, so Flint said."

They got out, put gloves on, and George tapped on the wood, idly considering what Flint was about to tell them. The bloke had come on in leaps and bounds over the last few months. No big jobs had come in, so Flint's true worth had yet to be tested, but he'd done well enough at his initiation.

Flint opened up and smiled. He'd perched sunglasses on the rim of a baseball cap.

"What the fuck's that on your *face*?" George asked him.

"Dark makeup and a beard. I had to disguise myself somehow because some colleagues were around. I wasn't meant to be where I was today. I've tied him up by the way." He stepped back to let them in.

A bearded man sat on the sofa with kettle flex around his wrists and toaster flex around his ankles, the toaster sitting on his feet. He stared up at them, eyes wide, a juicy shiner over his right eye, as purple as a plum. Flint must have given him a wallop. The familiar smell of McDonald's drew George's attention to a large bag on the desk.

"Uber delivered it," Flint said, "just in case you need to cover my back. I didn't let him see much of me."

George walked over there and poked around in the bag. Took out a going-cold Big Mac and unwrapped it. "I was only just saying how hungry I was."

Sofa Man watched, clearly stumped for words that George was eating his order. He continued munching as if he wasn't there and this little gathering was of no importance. Flint sat beside the fella, browsing on his phone.

Food scoffed, George used a napkin to wipe his hands and face. He leaned his back against the wall opposite the sofa, arms folded. "Okay, sunshine, tell me all about it."

"I don't know what he's on about." The man jerked a thumb at Flint. "He's guffing on about some teen site or other, and I've never heard of it."

George glanced at their copper. "What's his name?"

"I don't know his real one, but he's called Amateur_Photographer on London Teens." He went on to explain Operation Balustrade, plus a police sting today, one that had gone wrong because they'd let this prick walk away. "To be fair, there were a lot of people there and not enough officers to keep an eye on everyone. I'd been watching him for a fair while. He just seemed weird, shifty, and when he used his phone, Anaisha took hers out of her pocket. All right, it was a minute or so later, but still, it set off alarm bells. You learn to get a feel for people in my job, and I recognise a pervert when I see one. He was eyeing up all the young girls. He won't confess to Summer because he won't want to admit he's responsible for her death."

"So you're into minors, are you?" George walked over to pick up a McDonald's cup. He opened a straw and stuck it in the top. Sipped Coke. Reminded himself to take the cup with him when they left. He returned to his spot against the wall and raised his eyebrows at their captive to encourage him to start talking.

"I was there to meet a woman, okay? I've already told him this."

"And she stood you up?"

"Yeah."

"Who is she? What's her name?"

"I don't know. She was on a dating app."

"People who use dating apps have names in their profiles. What, you expect us to believe she didn't have one? Fuck right off." George glared at him. "Now, I trust this copper here, and as it seems you're not willing to tell us the truth, we're going to go somewhere where you will. My brother will take a photo of you, because I want to know who you are. I'm sure someone will recognise you once our people show it around." He addressed Flint. "Take his computer and phone and put them in the back of our van. Switch the phone off. Oh, and bring the cup."

Flint wandered off to unplug the computer. "This was being put back to factory settings when I got here."

"So you've got something to hide, despite claiming your innocence." Greg took the photo.

Amateur hung his head, likely plotting to get himself out of this mess. As they only had Flint's word that this bloke was a pervert, they'd go gently on him at first, but as soon as George was sure Flint had been right, he'd up the ante.

"Get up, moron," he said. "I'll untie you, then we're going for a little drive."

Chapter Fourteen

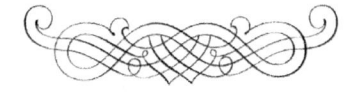

The twins' good friend, Laundrette Lil, had gifted them the use of a cottage set in seclusion at the edge of a forest. The windows, boarded up, prevented anyone from looking in, and inside it appeared like any other home — apart from a steel-lined room with a trapdoor in the floor. George had ordered for the place to be done up, all the old-fashioned furniture from the nineties replaced, the walls receiving a fresh coat of paint. It had once belonged to Ron Cardigan, their bastard sperm donor, so getting rid of everything he'd bought had been cathartic, not to mention it was a reminder to George that *they* ruled the roost here now, not him.

Captives could now be kept here, strung up in the steel room by chains attached to meat hooks in the ceiling, metal manacles around their wrists. Will, their usual babysitter, could stay here overnight instead of slumming it at the warehouse on the sofa. Saying that, George wasn't sure how quickly they'd kill their current victim, so Will might not be needed at all.

This was the first time the cottage was being used as a torture chamber by the twins. In the past, though, Ron had frequented it plenty of times, according to Lil. Skeletons lay beneath the building, where Ron had dragged the bodies of his targets. George hadn't gone below to investigate. He didn't fancy coming face to face with a pile of bones, not yet, especially as Ron had had a tendency to kill first, ask questions later. Some of the people down their had likely been innocent. But maybe it would be Amateur's final resting place, too.

It annoyed the shit out of George that their real dad had thought to create the steel room and they were now utilising it, but he wasn't that much of a ponce not to admire Ron's clever mind. This cottage was perfect for hiding dead people, and George wasn't about to cut his nose off to spite his face.

Prickly feelings for Ron aside, he knew a good thing when he saw it.

George and Greg had donned forensic suits, new gloves, and shoe covers. Amateur had been untied—they'd roped him up in the back of the van—stripped naked, and now hung from the chains, the manacles digging into his wrists. The nakedness was for humiliation, a way to get him to speak the truth faster. Maybe this bloke would walk free if he could prove he wasn't a pervert, but George didn't hold out much hope. Say what you liked about Flint, but he had good gut instincts, and he'd probably pegged Amateur correctly. Anyway, Amateur had a way about him that said he was hiding something. Behind his protests of not knowing what Flint was talking about lurked a man desperate to cover up his antics.

Most men who perved on minors would tend to lean that way. To hide what they'd done so they'd be freed to go and do it all over again. It must be like a drug, that need, or it was something inside them they couldn't ignore.

George had sent Flint off, he wasn't needed here. Greg was in the kitchen making a coffee using the barista machine George had bought—his obsession with a nice brew had leaked into all corners of his world, and if he had to drink instant or sub-par coffee, it often sent him into a bad mood.

A quick contemplation as to what to do with Amateur's body afterwards had George switching between letting him drop through the square in the floor and leaving him to rot beneath the cottage, or they could take him to the warehouse to cut him up and drop pieces of him in the Thames.

Maybe it was best to do it all here.

"What's your real name?" George asked Amateur for the seventh time—because he *was* counting, immature prick that he could sometimes be. "It's pointless not telling me, because like I said, our people will be showing your picture around, so someone's bound to tell us. They like to earn a bit of side cash, and fifty quid is fifty quid, right? All you're doing is delaying the inevitable by remaining silent—plus you're getting on my nellies, and honestly, that isn't advisable. Actually, fuck you and your zipped lips."

He accessed Marnie's number and sent the image to her. You never knew until you tried—don't ask, don't get.

GG: DO YOU KNOW THIS BLOKE?

Her response arrived quickly, and he read it.

What? Jesus fucking wept.

George walked out and went to the kitchen. "I've just shown Marnie the photo. It's Kendall fucking Reynolds, except he doesn't usually have a beard, only every now and again."

Greg stopped stirring a coffee. "What?"

"That was my first reaction, too, except there was a 'Jesus fucking wept' on the end."

"What a surprise."

"What are you referring to?"

"The Jesus fucking wept."

"Bloody Nora, you're confusing things. Just concentrate, will you? Did he grow that beard to disguise himself today? Has he done that in the past? And do we tell Ivory her husband's a sodding paedo or what?"

Greg pulled a face. "More to the point, what do we do now? If we kill him, make out he's gone missing, that's seven years until he's officially declared dead. She'd have to wait to claim anything of his. What if he's got savings stashed? She deserves to have it after what he's put her through." He slid a coffee cup towards George.

"I'll go and have another word with him in a sec, not that he'll say anything. He's being a stubborn little fanny."

Again, George thought about having to dump Kendall's body. Things had changed now, so he wouldn't be put under the floor *or* in the river. They were going to have to leave him to be found. Intact, more's the pity. That meant George couldn't have fun chopping him up. Janine was going to go spare when she found out Kendall was one of their targets, especially because leaving their usual note was really needed in this instance. He'd promised not to do that again, but how else could he get the point across that Kendall had played a part in Summer's death? If he didn't ask Ichabod to write it and didn't pop it in a sandwich bag like before, her colleagues might not voice their usual bollocks.

The solution on what to do with the body hit him, and he smiled.

"What's tickled you?" Greg asked.

"We'll kill him here and take him back to his garage. Let Janine know where his body is. She'll have to go down the anon tip-off route again."

"She's not going to like that. You know how antsy she's been getting because people—us—have been giving her information. It's going to look suspicious again, and her colleagues have already brought up the idea there's a vigilante out there. How long will it be before they realise she's linked to it all? Before they question why *she* keeps getting the tip-offs and not some other copper?"

"Then we'll tell Flint, let him deal with it. We *have* to have a body for Ivory's sake. And Remy's." George sipped some coffee. Bloody handsome.

Greg sighed, indicating he'd agreed to George's plan. "We'll need to wash the cunt before we dump him."

George frowned. "What?"

"Flint didn't have gloves on when he tied him up. He'd have touched his skin. We can't risk him getting caught via DNA being left behind."

"Then it's a good job we did what I suggested, isn't it. Another belter of an idea from me." George smiled, smug, because if they killed here, then transported their victims to the warehouse, he didn't want all that blood in their van or taxi. The steel room now boasted a tap and hose with a power-washer attachment on the end. Childishly chuffed *Ron* hadn't thought of that, he puffed his chest up.

Greg rolled his eyes. "Point made. You don't have to bang on about it."

"Admit it, I'm bloody clever."

"Whatever. So, Ivory? And then there's Terry to consider. We promised he could be with us when we sorted Summer's pervert. Do we want him knowing about this place? He's proved to us he can be trusted at work, but something like this?"

"We'll blindfold him when we pick him up. As for Ivory… Do you think she's in the right frame of mind to be here? Personally, I think just knowing he's responsible for Summer, plus he was going to meet what he thought was a thirteen-year-old today, well, it'd tip anyone over the edge. She just thinks he's a wanker of a husband who likes tormenting her. Isn't that enough?"

"Look, if you remember, we agreed to let all women at Haven have a voice, a say in what happens to their abusers once we've dug up dirt on them. We can give Ivory some time to come to terms with who Kendall really is. Will can babysit him here for a day or two. But give her the option to process it. Don't try and force her to agree straight away. She's had enough of that from her husband."

George couldn't argue with that. "Right, so we'll go and have a word with him, reveal we know who he is, then go from there."

He took his coffee into the steel room and sat on a metal foldout chair opposite Kendall, Greg doing the same. For a few sips they remained silent, staring at him. Kendall stared back to begin with, but the intensity finally got to him, and he hung his head.

"What's Marnie like in the sack?" George asked.

Kendall's head snapped up. "Who?"

"Don't give me all that 'who?' bollocks. Marnie Fields, the woman you've been hooking up with behind your missus' back. You know, your *wife*, Ivory Reynolds."

Kendall narrowed his eyes. Sighed. "Fuck's sake."

"Do you want to explain yourself now? Even if you had nothing to do with Summer and that woman copper Flint mentioned to you, we'll wreck your reputation so badly that you won't want to show your face in your neck of the woods again. Just the way you treated Ivory and Remy is revolting; it's enough for us to ruin your life. Actually, we've killed for less, so what's the point in taking your secrets to your grave? Are you the type to be remorseful now you know you're near the end? Do you feel any guilt whatsoever?"

"You're going to kill me." A statement, so he'd got the gist.

"Yes, so you can't hurt Ivory or Remy again. It's for the best."

Kendall thought for a moment. "I had nothing to do with that Summer girl, all right?"

"Who *did* you have something to do with?"

"Girls, ten of them."

George hid his disgust—and his surprise that Kendall was prepared to open up like this. Maybe he *would* be remorseful after all. *Makes a change.* So many people they'd dealt with went down the 'fuck you' route, covering up any real feelings of regret on some misaligned mission to show they were hard nuts right to the last knockings, that George and Greg standing in front of them didn't bother them one bit.

Men and their egos…

"And what did you do with them?" George asked, although he dreaded the answer. Just knowing girls were involved was enough to churn his stomach and invite anger to come out to play.

"I handed them over to clients. Men ordered them, I delivered."

George stood and chucked his coffee in Kendall's face. "Are you telling me you picked up minors for *perverts*? Off your own bat? Or are you working for a bigger organisation?"

Kendall blinked the liquid away, making a good show of disguising how the coffee must have stung his eyes and burnt him. "It's my business, what I do for a living. I set it up on the dark web. People will pay you to do anything.

There are killers, hitmen, women prepared to do honey traps, porn rings, you name it. There's a whole depraved world under the surface."

"And you're okay with that?"

"The girls were a payday, nothing more."

"How did you even stumble on all that? The dark web?"

"A bloke I knew showed me. We were about eighteen, bored and fucking about."

"Who is this bloke?"

"He's dead. Shot himself."

George believed him, relieved they wouldn't have to go after the wanker for introducing Kendall to the darkness. "These girls, their parents think they've just gone missing?"

"Some of them, yeah. A few have turned up. The bodies. Their parents know their daughters were killed—the police worked out who they were."

"What the fuck planet are you on where you think that's remotely okay?"

"Look, if I tell you everything, I swear to God I won't do it again. I've booked a flight to Spain. I'm fucking off."

"You're fucking off all right, but Hell's your destination, my old son." George walked over to a wall and smacked the cup against it. The china broke, leaving the handle and a pointed shard in his hand.

Greg glared at him. "Those cups cost twenty quid each, bruv. Fucking hell."

"I don't give a toss." George faced Kendall and stabbed the shard into the bloke's dick.

The resulting scream fuelled one of George's alters, and Mad came to the fore, begging him to wrench that shard out and stab this fucker all over, turning him into a sieve.

"You," he said, when Kendall had piped down, "are a filthy, nasty little cunt. What was the point in the envelopes?"

"I-I don't know anything…about any…envelopes." Kendall's eyes watered, tears streaming down his face. His dick bled around the shard, droplets hanging on the end then dripping off.

"The ones you got Summer to leave in bins."

"Seriously, I don't know what…what you're on about."

His panting was getting on George's tits. "Breathe properly, you stupid munter."

Kendall attempted to get himself under control.

"Tell me about the one you were meeting today—who you *thought* she was."

"She said she was thirteen. She sent me a picture, and she fitted what one of the clients had asked for."

"Who's the client?"

"I don't know. I name them by numbers. He's Client 10."

"How do they pay you?"

"Bank transfer. Offshore account. Expenses then a mil at the handover."

"You had it all worked out, didn't you. I have to say, if you weren't a wife-beating paedo, I'd admire your business sense. But you *are* a wife-beating paedo, so I feel nothing but contempt towards you. Everything will be on that computer hard drive, despite you thinking you've wiped it, so we'll get to the truth in the end."

Kendall smirked. "It won't. I buy a new computer for each girl, so all you'll have is the most recent one."

Clever fucker. "Why didn't you wait for today's girl to show up?"

"She was giving me the runaround, fucking me about. I knew something was off when that

Flint bloke kept staring at me. I had to get out of there. Said to myself I'd give it up, just leave the country, then he showed up here. But I'm telling you, I did nothing to Summer. That's on someone else."

"I don't believe you."

"Believe whatever you like. I'm dead soon, so what do I care?"

Ivory sprang to mind, so George asked, "That offshore account. How much is in it? I think Ivory should have it, don't you?"

Greg got up. "I'll get his phone out of the van."

"Hang on, bruv." George followed him out of the room and shut the door. "If we switch it on… When his body's found, Janine and her team will poke into Kendall's life, his phone number especially, and work out his location at the points it was switched on and off. The last thing we need is coppers crawling all over this place, so we can't fire it up here. Get hold of Flint. He needs to run a check on whether this pleb here has a mobile contract."

Greg pursed his lips. "And how will Janine explain things when that search is flagged? No, we'll have to go somewhere in the van, take a route with no cameras, and access his phone there."

"We need him with us. He'll have facial recognition, I bet."

"Fuck's sake. Come on."

Together, they wrapped clingfilm around Kendall's arse and dick, creating a waterproof nappy so blood didn't transfer, hosed him off to get the claret from his cock off his legs, then took him down and bundled him into the van. Greg drove back to the garage, and George got out to get into the back. He brought the locked home screen to life and pointed it at Kendall. The phone unlocked, and George frowned at there only being two apps.

"Have you deleted everything else?"

"What's it look like?"

George gritted his teeth. "I don't like your attitude, and you're going to pay for being rude to me. Before that, though, we'll sort that money of yours. It'll go to our offshore account, and we'll make sure Ivory gets it in chunks, as if it's her wages and she works for us. She'll be down as a secretary at our casino, a nice little cover story."

Giving Ivory money that had been paid for girls seemed wrong, though.

He tapped the banking app and pointed the phone at Kendall again. George glanced at the total. Christ. Nine million plus a few hundred thousand. He appeared to pay himself about three grand a month into another account. Some had been paid out earlier today, back to someone who'd put the same amount into the account five months ago. Client 10 might well be traced, the same with the others, so leaving this phone with Kendall's body was the way to go. The police could solve the dilemma of who all the paedos were.

But then our offshore account could be traced. Maybe we should leave the money where it is. Give Ivory some compensation instead.

He switched to the contacts and checked the names. Clients one to ten. Kendall had kept their numbers, maybe as insurance so they wouldn't dare grass him up for procuring the girls?

We'll leave a note on his desk at the garage, as if he's written it.

He switched the phone off, got out, and returned to the passenger seat. They arrived at the cottage and strung Kendall up.

George turned to Greg. "I'll explain in a minute, but the money stays where it is."

Greg nodded.

George grinned at Kendall. "Change of plan. You hang tight." He laughed. "We'll be back later."

He left the room, loving how the shard was still sticking out of Kendall's cock inside that nappy, how it would bring pain every time he moved.

First stop was to Ivory, the second to Terry, and then justice would be served.

Chapter Fifteen

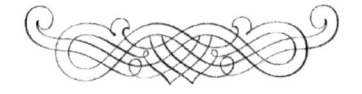

Ivory had slept well for the first time in years, although she'd woken up disorientated, thinking she was still at home. The last time she'd done that had been on holiday in the early days with Kendall. As soon as she registered the surroundings of her new en suite room, she'd relaxed and had a good cry, relief a powerful emotion, thanking whatever deity would listen that she was here, safe, and didn't have to face him today. No anxiety about him walking in after stopping out all night, or if he'd stayed in, no tiptoeing around him, those bastard eggshells waiting to crack beneath her tentative tread. God, she should have done this sooner.

Remy had slept in until ten, curled up on a single bed next to her double, likely exhausted as he'd had a big day yesterday, what with getting his new bike and wanting to ride around the huge back garden until way past his bedtime. Ivory had allowed it, seeing as he wasn't going to school today. Using the phone Sharon had given her courtesy of the twins, she'd rung the secretary first thing, saying he was poorly. Revealing what was actually going on wasn't something she wanted to do, not yet, not until she was aware of how the twins were going to proceed. She hadn't contacted Mum or her caseworker yet, unable to handle that at the moment. While she settled in here, she just wanted a bit of peace.

The morning had been spent chatting. Remy currently played in the garden with Tasha, sharing his bike with her, Ivory proud that he was such a good boy, when he could have turned into a little shit, considering what his home life had been like. Calista sat and watched them, baby Archie asleep in a pushchair.

Everyone here had been so kind to Ivory, and the family feel had shown her exactly what she'd been missing, a reminder that she'd had it once as a child and hadn't realised how blessed she'd been at the time. Guilt coiled in her gut that she hadn't provided the same safe space for her son, but she'd make up for it. Her home with Kendall was barren of warmth compared to this place, and to be able to speak out and share her story without reproach was worth its weight in gold. No one blamed her for staying with Kendall, they'd all done the same with their partners. Their minds had been so warped that staying had seemed safer than running. Better the devil you know than the one you didn't.

Now, Ivory faced the twins in Sharon's office so they could talk to her without the other women listening. Yes, she'd told the ladies everything, and maybe she'd share this with them afterwards, but when it came to finding out what was going to happen to Kendall, she'd prefer to be with The Brothers by herself. That *was* why the twins were here, wasn't it?

"Kendall's been apprehended," George said, a coffee in front of him where he sat behind Sharon's desk, Greg next to him. "As it happens, he came to us in a quirk of fate. Our copper reckoned he was suspicious so followed him to a row of garages. He was inside one. Do you know anything about that?"

Confused, Ivory frowned. "Why would he have a garage? He parks his car at home."

"It's done up like a living space. Sofa, desk, even a little kitchen of sorts. No bathroom, though, so God knows where he went for a piss. You told us before that he stayed out overnight sometimes. My guess is it was there."

"I had no idea."

How could he have kept something like that from her? Then she backtracked—of *course* he could keep it from her. He had so many secrets lately, and he didn't share snippets of what he got up to anymore. They'd lost the art of proper conversation, and now it was a case of him barking orders, putting her down, or shouting obscenities in her face.

Had he taken Marnie there? Was that where they'd—

Ivory couldn't get her head around this. "Does he rent it or something?"

"No, our private investigator's been looking into him. He owns it."

"But where would he have got the money from to buy it? Is there a mortgage?"

"This is the bit that will upset you. He's coined it in, but he isn't a brickie, and he earned his money in a nasty way. Looked to me like he lived off the interest. Has he ever showed signs of looking at little girls?"

Ivory's blood ran cold. "What? No! What are you implying?"

George explained something so horrific she forgot to breathe for a moment. Kendall, sourcing young girls for men? What? And those parents, not knowing where their children were for years, and some of them being told they'd been found dead, abused? Who *were* these bastards?

"How is that even possible?" she asked, nauseated. "He comes home from work covered in brick dust. It gets in his hair and everything. I moan to myself all the time about having to wash his filthy clothes." She didn't want to believe the twins, so was that why she made excuses?

Bringing things up to prove Kendall wasn't what they'd said he was?

"We haven't had a proper root around in his garage, but I suspect there'll be a bag of cement or something like that, maybe in one of the kitchen cupboards. He likely throws it on himself, because I'm telling you, he isn't a brickie."

"Has he admitted to that?"

"Yes."

Her stomach plummeted. "And the other thing, those girls?"

"Yes. He's got over nine mil in the bank. He sells *people*, Ivory, like someone else would sell sweets. He came off as thinking it was normal, just a way to make money."

She shook her head. "He can't have that much. He said we were skint."

"I've seen it for myself in his offshore account. Much as I'd like to send the cash to you, it's going to lead straight to us if anyone at the bank follows the trail—or the police do. It's dirty money, paid by filthy paedos."

For a moment, she imagined having it, living the life, never worrying, giving Remy the best upbringing, but no, she couldn't take it. "I wouldn't want it anyway. I don't care what happens to it." There, she'd said it, so there was no taking it back now.

"You'll be compensated by us, though. You've been through a lot, and the money we'll give you will help you back on your feet, plus some can go towards a funeral once the police release his body after their investigation."

A part of her mourned the man Kendall used to be, the one she'd loved, the one who'd loved her, but the other part rejoiced that he couldn't hurt anyone ever again. How had he slept at night? How had he got involved in something so awful? Did she even want to know? They said ignorance was bliss.

"He's dead?" she asked.

"Not yet. We were waiting to see whether you wanted to be there before we did anything. We usually offer the wronged party a chance to stand and watch or actually do the killing. Is that something you want?"

"I've imagined doing it plenty of times, but…no."

"Terry Meeks will be asked if he wants to be there, too. I think he deserves a front-row seat when Kendall is sorted. Maybe his wife an' all."

"I can't face them. I can't be there, not after what my husband did to their daughter. I'd rather you just do it and the police come here to speak to me afterwards."

"But they won't know where you are. For this to look legit, you'll have to go home. Say you slept here last night because you're our cleaner, some shit like that, and you finished late so stayed over. Sharon and the others will back you up, but you need that alibi. The police are going to dig into his life, and all it would take is one neighbour to say they'd heard him walloping you, all that shouting, and you'd go straight to the top of the suspect list. We can't let that happen."

"What about Remy, though? He thinks he doesn't have to go home again. He'll think I lied to him."

"Do you *want* the police suspecting you?"

"No! I never want to live in that house again, but I'll go back for a couple of nights if I have to."

"Would Remy be okay staying with your mum? We'll likely be dumping the body overnight, and Kendall will be found in his garage after a tip-off. Hopefully, the police will pop round yours first thing, then you can make a show of phoning Sharon to say you won't be able to make it into work. Do you think you can pull it off, the shock when the pigs say he's been murdered?"

"I'll have to, won't I. I told the school he was poorly, so him being at Mum's won't look weird—I'll tell the police she offered to watch him while I went to work, but of course, I won't be going because I haven't even got a fucking job."

"Then say you're off out for the night. Right, we'll drop you off round your mum's using the van. We'll even tell her what's going on if you like."

Ivory nodded, taking the easy route. If the twins explained, Mum wouldn't give her much grief, she'd accept this was the way it had to be. Her 'I told you so' recriminations could wait for another day.

"Can we take Remy's bike?"

"Yeah, it can go in the back of the van with you two."

Telling Remy they were leaving could go one of two ways: him kicking up a stink or being pleased they were going to Nanny's. She didn't want him upset any more than he already had been, so in order to work out how to word it to him, she asked, "Can I just have a few minutes alone to process what you've told me? It's a lot."

George nodded. "It is, and we get it. We'll leave you to it and get hold of Terry. We'll be in the kitchen."

She watched them leave, then broke down, trying to come to terms with the fact she'd been living with a man who'd supplied girls to perverts.

How the *fuck* hadn't she seen that trait in him?

Chapter Sixteen

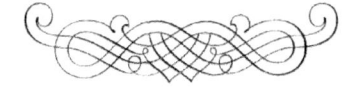

Part of life was to endure grief and weather storms, but Anaisha was sick of the stagnancy, how only she seemed to be the one moving forward in all areas. Dayton wouldn't want her moping around, so she refused to be unhappy all the time, preferring to hide any sorrowful moments when they snuck up on her unannounced. She was going mad living at home, too.

To be fair, Mum was slowly smiling more, laughing sometimes, but Dad had remained stuck in place, his scowl still there. Janine and Grace popped in regularly—the case had obviously got to them back then if they kept coming here to check on them, and besides, friendships had formed, more so after Anaisha had joined the police.

Janine was instrumental in getting Mum to see a life where she could still grieve but be upbeat every now and then, too. She'd suggested a support group, which Mum actually attended, surprising Anaisha. She came back happier, as if whatever was spoken about there had lifted a weight off her shoulders. There was *a future after the death of a loved one, you just had to find it, find that comfortable nook where you still mourned but it wasn't such a heavy cloak anymore.*

If only Dad could see that.

Or was Anaisha being a cow? Not everyone could file their grief away into a convenient box. Like Mum had said on the worst night of their lives when Quint and Raquel had come round, "We all cope in different ways."

Anaisha should cut her father some slack, especially as it was his son who had died, not his brother. It must be horrendous to lose a child. Still, she was being suffocated by what felt like a dense atmosphere, the air at home thick with tension and sadness. For her to get through her own mourning process, she needed some light amidst the dark.

It was likely time for her to move out despite the guilt she'd feel by doing it. She hated the thought of Mum and Dad feeling like they'd lost her, too, when she wasn't under their roof, but remaining there would be damaging to her mental health, especially as they thought her visits to Shaq meant she breathed the same oxygen as the enemy, therefore, she was a traitor. Why didn't they understand what she was doing by going there?

Thankfully, as well as having Grace to talk to, she'd met someone, a copper who used to be at the same station as her. Ben had left a couple of years ago. She'd noticed him when he'd worked there—hard not to when he was so charismatic and magnetic—but he was older than her and married at the time. Now he was divorced, and she'd bumped into him outside the station a year ago while he'd been talking to Edgar Nelly, one of his old copper mates. Ben had asked her if she wanted to go for a drink. He'd said it like he'd meant it as a joke and had later confessed he'd done that in case she'd knocked him back in front of Edgar and the jest angle would save him any embarrassment.

Right from the start of their relationship, she'd explained about Shaq, Dayton, and her parents, and how she felt powerless to help Mum and Dad. They'd had the same discussion recently, and Ben had asked her to move in with him. He'd suggested her parents may need space, that they might secretly resent her for being alive when Dayton wasn't, and that maybe distance was the answer. It hadn't upset her, what he'd said, because she'd considered it herself, under no illusion that Dayton was the golden child and always had been, but she'd never hated him, or them, for it. Sometimes you just liked someone more than others, no explanation for it.

She had to tell them she was moving out, and she wasn't looking forward to it. What if Ben's prediction wasn't right and they begged her to stay? Could she? Was it fair of them to ask her to remain in a place where the walls were closing in on her? To be honest, the memories the family home contained were killing her inside. Every corner held a part of Dayton, even down to the dining table in the kitchen where he'd spilled turps on it and the varnish had come off.

Her parents liked Ben, so that was one hurdle sorted. Now, she just had to jump over the others without accusing them of wallowing in their grief or blaming them for her state of mind and her need to get away from them. Mourning wasn't one size fits all, and they had to understand that her brand of it didn't match theirs and that was okay.

She took a deep breath, slid her key in the lock, and entered the house.

Here goes…

A week later, while Anaisha waited for Shaq to be let into the visiting hall, she mulled over how Mum and Dad had taken the news. Surprisingly well, although there had been tears when she'd packed some of her things, put others in boxes in the loft, and vacated the house the next day. Still, it was done, and she could breathe now. Ben was attentive and kind, everything she'd hoped for in a partner, and at last, life was looking a lot better.

She sipped her coffee, thinking about her approach with Shaq today. Maybe she shouldn't bother asking him if he was sorry—he'd be expecting it, and he'd have a spiteful answer all lined up, so perhaps switching things up would get the results she wanted.

The far door opened, and he walked towards her, then sat and reached for one of the cakes. No hello, just accepting she'd bought them for him. Did he look forward to these visits so he could remind her, every time, that he'd taken her brother away? Did it give him pleasure?

He finished the cake and picked up his coffee. Drank some. Eyed her over the rim. "No barking the usual question at me? Blimey, colour me shocked."

She shrugged. "How have you been?"

"What do you care, copper?"

She'd told him she'd joined the force ages ago, and he'd mocked her for it, saying she was a walking cliché, wanting to right the wrongs because of a life trauma. He'd laughed at her, taunted her, but it didn't hurt. How could it when he'd done it so often in the past? When she expected it?

"I was asking to be polite. You know, to show you how normal people behave."

"You shouldn't care how I am."

"I don't, not in the usual sense. Maybe I should have asked it a different way: do you still hate it in here? Do you wish you weren't locked up?"

"Who says I hate it?"

"Don't you, though?"

He seemed about to say something but changed his mind. "I'm not explaining my feelings to you."

"I doubt I'd understand them anyway."

"You've got that right. You've never been oppressed."

Was he hinting that he had? Did he want her to press him on it?

"Are you for real?" she asked. "You oppressed me. You were cruel to me sometimes when I was with Dayton."

"Not in the same way I suffered." He grabbed another cake.

"Want to talk about it?"

"No. You of all people wouldn't get it."

"What do you mean by that?"

"Look, some people do things because they can't help it. There's something inside them that makes them do shit."

"Are you going to tell me you hear voices and that's why you killed my brother?"

"Something like that, just not the voices you mean."

She frowned. "Whatever." His games got on her nerves, yet still she visited.

Ben was likely right. She should stop coming. She wasn't getting what she needed by being here, and she only fuelled Shaq's need to be spiteful to her.

She decided to be spiteful first. "You won't be let out for another two decades if you don't get the thumbs-up from the parole board, and you'll have missed the best years of your life. No girlfriend or kids. No job. No holidays or whatever."

"I made my choice. I ensured I was put in here for a reason."

He was cryptic like that sometimes and never explained what he meant, so she wouldn't bother prompting him to. She was getting to know him more with each visit, and he never offered insights if she pushed for them. Better to just let them come out naturally. She reckoned that deep down he was dying to open up to her; he needed someone to talk to but couldn't bring himself to show his softer side.

"I've got a boyfriend," she said. "I moved in with him last week. Life is so good." She enjoyed goading him. "If you thought you'd break me by killing Dayton, you got it so wrong."

"Is he black or white?"

"Who, Ben?"

"Yeah."

"What does that matter?"

"It doesn't."

Why had he bothered asking, then?

She sighed. "Then you won't mind if I don't answer."

Anger warped his features. He ate the last cupcake. Finished his coffee. "What does he do?"

"He's a police officer."

"Does he know about me?"

"Yes."

"And how fucked-up you are over everything?"

"I'm not fucked-up."

"You should be."

"Why would I allow that to define me when it would make you happy? I smile because you want me to be sad. I laugh because it proves you didn't beat me."

"Your dad's stull gutted."

"I suppose your mum or dad told you that."

"Yeah."

"Have you at least apologised to them for ruining their lives?"

"I haven't ruined them, I saved them."

His mysterious snippets got on her nerves, but she wouldn't show it. "So becoming a murderer saved your parents? That doesn't make sense."

"It would if you know the full story."

"So tell it. Get it off your chest."

"Nah."

She sighed again. "I'd better go. Back to my perfect, lovely little life, leaving you to your imperfect shitty one."

"Before you go, I'm still not sorry." He smirked.

"I didn't expect you to be. Bastards like you never are. I doubt I'll come here again. You don't deserve my company, the coffee, or the cakes."

A flicker of alarm crossed his features.

"What's the matter?" she asked. "Are you upset I'll be depriving you of being able to play your sick games with me? They're boring, you're boring, so there isn't any point in me being here."

"I thought you wanted to reform me."

"What's the point? You'll never change." She stood. *"See you."*

She walked away, chuffed she'd got under his skin.

"You'll be back," he called after her. "You can't help yourself."

She ignored him and left the room. But he was right, she would be back. She'd get a sorry out of him if it was the last thing she did.

Chapter Seventeen

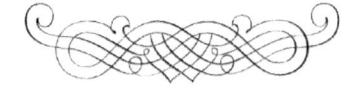

Parked outside one of the other shops the twins protected, Terry sat in the passenger seat, Martin beside him. Staring out on the road ahead, at the people who wandered around living their lives, he wished he was them. To not have anything more pressing than going from A to B, getting shit scrubbed off a to-do list. To walk into that shop and buy bits and bobs for dinner, maybe a magazine to read this afternoon while drinking tea and dunking chocolate Hobnobs, telling himself off for eating the whole packet. To not have this heavy weight that had suddenly encroached on him, heavier than he'd imagined it would feel.

He hadn't appreciated that life until it had disappeared. Hadn't realised how *lucky* he was to think his world was duller than ditchwater and that he was stagnating, stuck in a marriage with a grumpy missus and a daughter who'd rolled her eyes at him more often than not, making it clear she only tolerated him. He'd lost his job at the factory, his purpose, and had experienced the urge to walk away from it all and not look back.

How he wished he was back there now, bored, nothing better to do than moan about how being an adult wasn't all it was cracked up to be. That life was infinitely better than his current one. What was it they said? You don't know what you've got till it's gone.

He was about to commit murder, or he would be later, and the prospect of that didn't feel as euphoric as he'd imagined. Terry was what some would call a waste of space, but he had feelings, and he did have *some* morals, no matter what people thought. To actually know damn well he *was* going to take a life was far more unsettling than just thinking about it, toying with the scenarios. He should be over the moon, but his conscience had decided to pipe up. The paedo might have a mother, father, maybe siblings, people who loved him, and Terry was going to take that all away, plunge them into the hell he inhabited, where they'd never see their loved one again. Just because he suffered, and Willow, did it mean *they* had to?

Was death really the way to get justice?

He'd just received a call from George. Anger had burned so hot he'd sweated, and he'd struggled to breathe properly. Now, though? He was at sixes and sevens. Confused. Wondering whether he should step back and let the twins deal with this for him. George hadn't helped, he hadn't answered any of Terry's questions. Should that worry him? Why wouldn't he say who the bloke was?

Fuck, do I know him?

He wasn't sure how to feel about that. If one of his friends or neighbours had done this... Maybe that was why George had refused to reveal the paedo's identity. Wasn't it better that Terry found out when he clapped eyes on him? The rage that would undoubtedly surge at the perv's betrayal would come in handy. If he knew now, he'd waste all that violent energy prior to facing him.

"What's happened?" Martin asked.

"They've found him."

Martin didn't ask what Terry had meant, he'd likely realised all by himself. Like Terry had thought before, Martin was perceptive, or maybe they were just that in tune. It was like that sometimes, wasn't it. You met someone who read between the lines, who heard what you *didn't* say. They gelled with you, and there was no explanation for it. Terry had once had that sort of relationship with Willow, but their bond had burned out, only ashes remaining. Would she leave him once the pervert was dead? Was she only hanging on to the last vestiges of their marriage because Terry was a link to Summer, the person who'd promised her he'd find him, end him?

While he could admit their partnership would never be the same again, surely they could salvage it, form a different kind of alliance in their new, harrowing, excruciatingly awful reality. He wasn't sure he could cope without Willow in his corner. She'd been there for so long, Terry sometimes forgot she existed, but if she wasn't there, it would be so apparent, so *empty*, that he'd break down. They might not get on anymore, her seemingly only stomaching his presence, but they were bound together by grief, the years of bringing Summer up, and their time before she'd been born, so that had to count for something.

They couldn't just throw it all away.

"What's happening now?" Martin opened the window, perhaps sensing Terry needed some fresh air.

Grateful for the cool breeze soughing through, Terry wiped sweat off his face. "They've asked me whether Willow would want to be there when…" He rubbed his forehead. "I had a blip just now—wasn't sure if I could go through with it. And I don't know if she will. She's a different person lately, so I can't predict what she'll say. She used to be so fiery, but it's like the spark's gone out of her."

"Understandable. She's lost her only child."

"Her reason for living, you mean."

Terry didn't blame her for that. He'd felt the same way to begin with. Summer's suicide had thrown him for a loop, and he hadn't been able to think of a single reason to stay alive—even Willow hadn't been enough to stick around for. The only thing that kept him going now was his mission to find the paedo. Since the twins had done that, what would be left afterwards? Later today, when the bloke was dead, would there be any reason to continue with this shitty life? For either of them? The shared drive that bound them together these days would be gone. What was there once justice had been served? When Willow's love for him had so clearly been snuffed out, why would she stay with him?

It scared him to think about it.

Terry pushed those thoughts aside. He could deal with it all another day, but he had an awful feeling that he and Willow would go the same way as their daughter. They'd take pills with booze and shut their eyes for the last time.

"George said I need to get back to them sharpish because they want to come and pick me up. I'd better ring the wife." He took his phone out, hovering his thumb over the keypad that had sprung up on the screen, hesitating on plugging in the PIN to unlock it.

Fuck it, I'll just say it outright. Me beating around the bush will only naff her off.

He rang her.

She picked up quickly, saying a breathy, "Terry?" as if she'd run somewhere private to answer the call.

"They've got him."

"Oh my fucking *God*..."

Sobs filtered into his ear, so he pressed the phone tighter to it, mindful that she wouldn't want Martin listening to her grief. Even if she didn't know Terry wasn't alone, he'd still give her this courtesy. It sounded as if she struggled to breathe, the same as his reaction. He wished he could shield her from it, all this, but then again, she deserved to feel the relief, to know this part of their hideous journey would soon come to an end.

"What...what happens next?" she whispered.

"They want to know if you need to be there when they...when they kill him."

"Oh shit. Oh God, I don't know. Do I?"

He felt for her. So many thoughts must be going through her mind. He had no doubt she'd do anything for Summer, but maybe she was afraid of who it would turn her into—a raging maniac—and she didn't want to see another side of herself, adding it to the other ones she'd been since they'd lost their child.

He let out a slow breath. "Only you can answer that, love."

"Are you…? Will you…?"

He knew what she wasn't saying, and it made his mind up for him. That blip was just that, a blip. He wouldn't renege on his promise to her. "You don't need to ask me that. I'm going to be the one killing him. I told you I would, and I won't back down. Can you handle that now it's come down to the wire? Can you cope with knowing I did it?"

"Yes. Kill that bastard for our Summer."

Goosebumps sprouted on Terry's arms at the vehemence in her tone, and he'd swear he knew exactly how she was feeling. Angry, utter vengeance swarming through her body, the need for that man to understand what he'd done to their girl, to them. How he'd ensured they were going to live a life of hell.

"I'll make sure he suffers," he said. "Where are you?"

"At work, where else?"

Willow had eventually chosen her job as a crutch over the booze, and she'd become a workaholic, doing overtime more than was good for her. Maybe she couldn't stand being at home where the memories of happier times stared at her from the photos on the walls, where Summer's laughter didn't ring out anymore, where there was only a table setting for two instead of three. Or maybe she couldn't stand spending much time with him, still secretly blaming him for everything. That last one was all too true. She didn't look at him if she could help it. Perhaps she worried she'd see recrimination in his eyes, how she'd have to face the fact *she* was just as responsible for not stopping Summer from using that fucking laptop.

It was a bitter pill, to know you'd failed. That if you'd just got brave and opened your mouth, you'd have changed the course, changed the future.

"Stay there," he said. "Do another shift. Get a taxi home, don't walk. You'll need an alibi. The more people who see you the better."

"Okay. Let me know when it's done—and ring, don't text me."

His usual retort would be that he wasn't stupid, he knew not to write anything down, something that could be used against him later, but he held it inside. What she'd said proved she cared whether he got the blame for this, or perhaps she was more concerned that *she* didn't. An uncharitable thought, but with her changing so much, he had no clue what went on inside her head anymore.

"But what about you?" she said. "Where will you say you've been?"

Terry glanced across at Martin. He wouldn't ask the bloke to cover for him, not when they drove all over the place and the car would be captured by cameras. As much as Martin tried to avoid them, it wasn't possible everywhere. Footage would show Terry hadn't been in the car, and he'd be up shit creek.

A solution popped into his mind. It wasn't the best, and it had been born out of desperation, but it meant many people would see him, and that was what he needed. "Listen, can you handle people thinking I went to see someone behind your back?"

"What do you mean?"

"I could say I was in the massage parlour at The Angel for the evening. I reckon George and Greg will make sure the women there say that's where I was. I'd need to check with them about it first, but if it's something you'd be uncomfortable with, I'll have to think of another place to be. I don't want you dealing with any extra shit."

"What extra shit? What does it matter if you get a massage? It could be for a bad back, for fuck's sake."

"It might come out in the press once the police hear my alibi. A lot of people know it isn't just a massage parlour."

"What?"

"Sex is sold there, love, but it's on a need-to-know basis."

She didn't even ask how he knew that. At one time it would have been the first question out of her mouth, and she'd have accused him of going there, paying for sex, but considering what they'd been through, that kind of thing just didn't matter anymore. And he only knew about it because he worked for the twins. He'd been oblivious prior to that, because Terry might be many things, but he wasn't a cheater. He'd never fuck about behind Willow's back like that.

She tutted. "Our daughter is dead. What could be more horrific? I can cope with *anything* else now, nothing is worse than that. If people think you're having it away with prostitutes, let them. Do what you have to do, just make sure you're not implicated. I…" She paused. "I love you, Terry."

Fuck, his eyes stung. He'd thought she'd fallen *out* of love with him, so to hear that… They were going to be okay, weren't they?

He cleared his throat. "I love you, too. Look, if it comes to the police poking into our phones, I rang just now to check on you, okay? Because of what we've been through, that should fly."

"What did we talk about?"

"Summer. Our feelings. How to move forward."

"Right. Right. Go. Do it. *Hurt* the fucker."

The line went dead.

Terry leaned his head back and closed his eyes. She still loved him, and that would get him through. There was a speck of hope now, that they'd be all right, after a fashion, once that bastard was killed. They could weather whatever fate threw at them—Willow was right, nothing trumped their Summer being dead. Nothing.

He turned to Martin. "Sorry for fucking up your schedule, I just need to ring the twins back."

"Don't apologise. This is more important than picking up poxy money."

Terry switched from his personal phone to his work burner.

George answered with a, "What's the verdict?"

"She's not coming. It's better she stays at work and is seen." Terry suggested the parlour as a way to keep himself safe.

"Good idea. Get Martin to drop you there now. Have a pint at the bar. Talk to people. Tell them you're going out the back because you've booked one of the women. You've got sciatica or some shit. I'll let Amaryllis know the score, and she'll pass it on to the girls and Belladonna—she's the lady on reception in the evenings. We'll come and pick you up, reverse the van down the side so no one will spot you getting in the back. We'll need to blindfold you, though."

It stung a little, that they didn't trust him with the destination, but maybe it wasn't that. Maybe it was a case of the least he knew the better and they were protecting him. The police *were* going to speak to him, he'd be at the top of their suspect list, so if he didn't know the location of the kill site, he couldn't slip up, could he.

"I understand. See you soon."

George cut the call.

Terry sighed. "The Angel."

Martin started the engine. "Do you need to talk anything through on the way?" He eased out of the parking spot and got going.

Terry told him the lot, all of his feelings, something he wouldn't have done a few months ago. "I'm finally going to get my hands on the bastard."

"I'm warning you, what you'll see might finish you off. George is…"

"I know what George is."

"I mean, I'm squeamish, and seeing what they do to people, it might upset you."

Terry laughed. "What *they* do? Mate, *I'm* the one who's going to be torturing that wanker. *Me*. I've got so much anger stored up he won't know what's hit him." He stared out of the side window. "He'll wish he'd never been born."

Chapter Eighteen

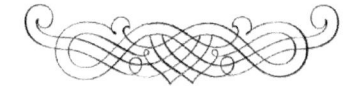

Everyone's mood had dipped once it had become clear that Amateur wasn't hanging around at the meeting spot—if he'd even really been there. On the way back to the station, Anaisha had contemplated that maybe he'd been toying with her, making out he was going to the cinema with her, when in fact, he had no intention of it. Now, she didn't know what to think.

They'd left the location at around three o'clock, staying until then just in case Amateur had still loitered, but no one had appeared suspicious to the rest of the team at the time. However, Fay and two others had been trawling through CCTV footage from outside the Odeon, which had revealed what the others had missed. Anaisha had spotted it while out in the field, though, and she was proud she had. Maybe she was good at this detective lark after all. Onscreen, two men were as off as she'd suspected them to be. Mr Beard and the man she'd spotted leaning on the wall, the one she'd mistaken for Flint.

"As we can see, they clearly interacted," Oliver said at the end-of-day briefing. He pointed to the screen that showed Wall Man. "He lifts his sunglasses and jerks his head at the gentleman sitting outside Costa, although 'gentleman' might be too a nice a term for him if this is what I think it is. My take on it? These two have probably been taking it in turns to speak to Anaisha online and they both arrived to collect her. When they didn't see her, they aborted the mission."

He clicked PLAY on two screens side by side displayed on the interactive whiteboard, one showing Wall Man leaving, the other showing Mr Beard doing the same. Anaisha toyed with admitting she'd thought they were weird earlier, but that would make her look a novice—she should have passed on her feelings the moment she'd experienced them, and Oliver would say as much, perhaps even blame her, because if he'd been alerted, those men wouldn't have got away. But there hadn't been time to say anything, or so she convinced herself.

Oliver sighed. "If we're going with the belief that these two men are our targets, at least we know it wasn't a lad and that my instinct to keep chatting was the correct road to go down."

Was he trying to justify his decision to show Anaisha that her thoughts on abandoning the chat had been wrong? If so, she was glad he hadn't said it outright, singling her out by name when he'd mentioned it. Then again, he didn't have to. Everyone would likely know exactly what he was getting at.

Oliver continued. "The problem we now have is, will Amateur answer Anaisha's latest message, the one she sent when we arrived back here, asking if they're all good? Yes, he said he was pissed off with her, and yes, that could mean he'll take his time to respond as a form of control or punishment, but my main worry is that he'll ditch her and start on someone new. Did the Teens site owner get back to you, Vi?"

DC Violet Kosh, the officer who'd sat outside Costa pretending to be part of a couple, nodded. "Brandon sent a message just now. No VPNs have been used since Amateur's last message to Anaisha. He's got someone monitoring it. As soon as VPN use pops up, he'll let us know. He said he'll note the time et cetera in case it occurs when we're all off the clock. I'm interested to see if it's the same one or different. Different presents us with a dilemma, though. One, it could be Amateur switching his access route; two, it might be someone else; and three, Amateur could have switched to using the layman's route in accessing the site; he could take himself off to an internet café or use someone else's Wi-Fi, which would then make him look like the masses using a regular IP. However, Brandon said he'll also send through a list of IPs every hour so we can check who the users are."

Oliver rubbed the end of his nose. "Right, as there's nothing that can be done unless he contacts Anaisha again, go home, get some rest. It's been an annoying day to say the least—no one's fault, I'm just expressing my frustration that we weren't in control, the men were. I'll stay here, kip in my chair. Anaisha, don't respond to him via your burner phone this evening. You deserve a break from him, so if he gets in contact, I'll speak to him as if I'm you. Leave that mobile here."

She opened her mouth to protest, but he shook his head.

"I mean it, I want you completely rested in case he asks for another meet. If he does, I'll push for it to be tomorrow. Go on, all of you get a proper night's sleep."

Everyone rose, leaving the open-plan office. Anaisha followed them and collected her bag from her locker, glad to be getting out of there. For a while back there she'd felt responsible for the sting going tits up, but no, she'd done all she could. The fact she could have been speaking to two men gave her the creeps, though—Amateur had never sounded any different, she'd always thought it was just one person. And there was her, convinced it had been a kid, so she couldn't trust her instincts anymore anyway.

Stupid cow.

She drove home, anxiety spiking all the way there now she was flipping from one stressful part of her life to another. What mood would Ben be in? Would he even be back yet? He worked late some evenings, no distinct pattern to his hours. Still, not to worry. This was her last night in the flat, not that she'd tell him that. She *could* leave this evening, but that would mean he'd ask questions, probably get lairy when she told him they were over. Better that she waited until he'd left for work in the morning before she packed her cases. She'd write him a note, visit Shaq, then sort a flat of her own.

In the meantime, she'd decided to go back to her parents' house tomorrow, face the inevitable barrage of queries. She planned to lie and say that by living together, she and Ben had realised they weren't compatible. Shit happened, that kind of thing. Dad would be disappointed, he liked Ben, but little did he know, Ben was the last person he should give the time of day to.

Mind made up that she'd be meek and mild one last time, she entered the flat, taking a deep breath at the sight of Ben's work shoes butted up against the skirting board beside two pairs of his trainers. Shit, he was home. She kept her boots on in case he turned nasty and she had to make a run for it, and she cursed him; she shouldn't have to think that way, to plot two steps ahead in order to keep herself safe.

She wandered into the kitchen and hung her handbag strap over the back of a dining chair. Ben sat at the little table, a ready meal in front of him still in the plastic tray. Steam curled from what appeared to be macaroni cheese.

"How was your day?" she asked and immediately regretted it. Hadn't he said he didn't want to discuss the case he was on? Bloody hell, she should have just said hello. The problem was, she was still getting used to navigating their life together since he'd changed. She forgot sometimes that he could turn mean in an instant.

"Christ almighty, stop pressing for information," he snapped.

"I'm not, I was just making conversation." Again, she'd made an error, plus she'd deviated from the meek-and-mild attitude she'd sworn to have. She'd spoken back to him, something abusers didn't like. She was supposed to know her place.

How awful that it had come to her seeing him that way, but he *was* an abuser. She wouldn't put up with it, though. Stress at work was a lame excuse for the way he treated her, and she didn't deserve what he put her through.

Her anger spiked. *Dangerous.*

"Are you starting on me again?" He scowled at her.

Starting on you? It's usually the other way round, you gaslighting fucker. "Nope. I can't be bothered."

She was playing this all wrong but couldn't seem to rein herself in. She wasn't so repressed that she could stop herself from retaliating. He hadn't had enough time to successfully manipulate *all* of her feelings in order for her to behave how he wanted, and after the day she'd had, she was pig sick of men thinking they held all the cards.

"*What* did you say?" He pushed the macaroni cheese away and stood.

No, I'm not doing this. I won't be scared of him. "If you come anywhere near me, if you hit me again, I'll phone it in." She made eye contact, waiting for his usual sneer, his usual bullshit about their colleagues not believing he was the sort to lay a hand on a woman. "I've had enough, all right? You don't get to speak to me the way you do."

"I'll speak to you however I fucking well like."

"True, that's your choice, but it doesn't mean I have to listen."

D'you know what? Fuck this bollocks. I'm leaving now.

She walked out, going into their bedroom, the heat of anger sending her cheeks hot. She'd managed to drag a suitcase out from under the bed by the time he joined her. Hair wrenched from behind, she lost her footing; he dragged her backwards towards the living room. She scrabbled her heels for purchase on the floor, but they slipped on the laminate. The pain from her hair being held in his fist brought on tears. They streamed down her face, and she'd bet he thought she was crying.

Not for you. Not anymore.

Did it matter what he thought?

No.

He threw her on the sofa. She went into work mode, assessing the situation, the threat he posed, and rolled to the side right when he lunged for her. He flopped down where she'd been, his face squashed against the back cushion. She pushed herself off the furniture and rushed into the hallway. The thud of his footsteps meant she had little time, but she made it to the front door, twisting the Yale handle.

He grabbed her hair again, turned her around to face the kitchen doorway, and pushed her in the back. She barrelled forward, hands out to break her fall, and landed on her palms and knees, agony spearing up her thighs and wrists. His presence close behind had her crawling forward, desperate to get to the kitchen so she could find a weapon to defend herself. A rolling pin would be better—she couldn't risk being hauled over the coals at work if she used a knife, having to explain why she'd chosen that when she knew damn well only reasonable force was allowed.

She reached for the bottom drawer beside the sink unit, pulling it open, but he kicked it shut, trapping her fingers. She cried out—Jesus Christ, that hurt—and tried to take her hand away, but he planted his socked foot on the drawer front to prevent it from opening, keeping her hand pinned.

"You really are pissing me off," he said. "You always have to try your luck, don't you. No matter what I say, you have to defy me."

Now she knew the real reason why his ex-wife had left him, why she'd filed for divorce. It wasn't because of the bullshit story he'd told Anaisha, where the woman was a bitch and had treated him like shit, it was because of this. *This*.

He removed his foot.

Anaisha quickly stood, backing away until she bumped into one of the base units, and cradled her throbbing hand to her chest. She didn't think he'd broken her fingers, but they were puffy and bruised in between the knuckles, dents in the skin from the edge of the drawer. Her mind catalogued what she'd do once he'd stormed out, and the first was to take a picture of her hand, and she'd continue to take them as evidence as the bruising got worse. Then she'd phone Janine. Lodge a complaint. Press charges whether he thought their colleagues would pooh-pooh what he'd done or not.

He punched her in the stomach, and as she hadn't been on her guard enough, it had taken her by surprise. She automatically bent double, coughing, pain winding through her abdomen.

Then he went for it, thumping her everywhere, slapping at her, pulling her hair. Some of it ripped, and she stared at it sailing to the floor.

"You'd better be gone by the time I get back," he said. "We're done. I can't cope with your bullshit anymore."

My bullshit? she wanted to scream. *It's yours, you fucking arsehole!*

But she remained silent, refusing to go down the route of: *If you hadn't provoked him, none of this would have happened.* Because, fuck, *he* was the one who should have controlled himself. *He* should have taken a moment to process how he'd react. He'd opted for the wrong road, and now he'd pay for it.

He left the kitchen, and she moved to watch him slipping his shoes on. Shrugging into his suit jacket. He walked out, slamming the front door, and she legged it down the hallway to double-lock the Yale and slip the chain on, then drew the top and bottom bolts across.

Only then did she go to the full-length mirror beside the coats hanging on the wall and look at what he'd done to her. She couldn't go to her parents' house now. A split lip and a face full of bruises would tell them exactly what she'd been putting up with. Instead, she found her phone and pressed in the number of a woman who would do her best to see Ben was punished.

Janine Sheldon didn't take fools gladly, and Ben would wish he hadn't laid a hand on Anaisha now. She and Janine together? He was *so* fucked.

In a warped and twisted way, she was glad she'd goaded him. It meant fully exposing him for who he was—he'd never hit her this much in one go before—and hopefully, no other woman would be taken in by his charm in the near future. With any luck, he'd serve a custodial sentence for what he'd done tonight and in the past. Maybe his ex-wife would come forward and give a statement.

It was the least he deserved, and if karma was sweet, he'd be placed in a cell with someone he'd put away—a man who'd want revenge.

Janine arrived within ten minutes of the call. She took one look at Anaisha and entered the flat, going straight to the kettle in the kitchen. She checked the water level then flicked the switch. Anaisha sat at the table and stared at the congealing macaroni cheese, her whole face throbbing.

"I know Ben from when he worked at our station." Janine took two cups out of a cupboard. "I *knew* there was something iffy about him. Don't ask me how my arsehole radar is so good, but believe me when I say I've got a sixth sense about people. When you told me it was him you lived with, I was tempted to say something, but you told me you were happy. I wish I'd prodded you a bit more now."

Anaisha drew her attention from the cold food and smiled sadly at Janine. It hurt her poorly lip, and she grimaced at the spike of pain. Licked the cut. "When we talked about me being with Ben, I *was* happy."

"I think he's threatened by you."

"What?"

"Some men don't like their women to do better than them, and I'm telling you, you'll exceed him in the ranks. He knows it, that's why he's trying to put you down so you don't believe in yourself. Thank fuck you saw what he was up to before it was too late." Janine rammed teabags into the cups as if she wanted to murder them. "I'll take your statement then call this in. I suspect he'll just slope off to the pub, will he?"

"I assume so. He never says where he's been, and I don't ask. I used to, but not anymore. I will *not* say tonight was my fault, but I did rile him up. I could have been the good little girlfriend and kept my thoughts to myself, but I didn't. This is the result."

"Wanker." Janine made the tea and brought the cups over. She sat, taking her phone out. "I'm going to record this, saves you having to repeat it all, although I expect you'll have to do that anyway. Still…"

Anaisha nodded. She started from the first time Ben had hit her and finished on tonight. Just saying it all out loud made it seem so much worse than it was.

No, don't diminish what he's done. It sounds bad because it is.

Janine shook her head and switched the recording off. "I'm going to enjoy seeing him lose his job, because in an ideal world, that's what should happen. You said he told you no one would believe you, that he'd get away with it because he's such a nice bloke at work. That may be true for the station he's in, but not ours. You know we have zero tolerance when it comes to one of our own being a tosser. They're treated the same as any other criminal. We can't be seen to sweep this kind of thing under the carpet, not with the public watching. All the shit in the news about bad officers—he can't be allowed to get away with this else there'll be another public outcry."

Anaisha found this line of chat too suffocating; she'd said what she had to say and just wanted to curl up into a ball. But she had the rest of the night to get through, and another officer or two would ask her to go over it all again, even though it was on the recording. She now had a new respect for victims of crime, how they sometimes looked so *tired* when they had to repeat themselves.

She changed the subject to get it off herself. "What conclusion did you come to about the DV murder case you're on?"

"Self-defence, hands down. She opened up to me today about how much she'd been putting up with, and she showed me a diary she'd kept. I don't blame her one bit for killing him, so we've dropped the charge to manslaughter due to diminished responsibility. She snapped, couldn't take any more. Hopefully the jury will agree—

there has to be a trial because she's going with not guilty."

Anaisha shuddered. "I hate the idea of my private life being bandied about, everyone at work knowing." She realised too late she'd brought the attention back to herself.

"There *is* another way of dealing with this." Janine sipped some tea then sat back and rubbed her tummy. "Although you don't strike me as the type to go down an illegal route in order to get what you want—for example, Ben being dealt with outside of court."

What is she saying? I need to be careful here in case she just means we come to an agreement with him that he doesn't go near me again. He pays me compensation or something. There's no way she's like me, is there?

Anaisha narrowed her eyes. "What are you getting at?"

"What I'm about to say goes no further."

"Okay…"

"If you blab, you'll regret it."

Anaisha swallowed. This sounded ominous. "I'll pretend the conversation never took place. You've done a lot for me and my family, and I'd never get you in any shit."

"Fair enough." Janine assessed her then nodded. "You've heard the rumours about The Brothers, right?"

Anaisha's stomach flipped. "Bloody *hell*, Janine!"

The DI shrugged. "It's an option. *If* the rumours are true, of course."

Why had she stressed the *if*? Didn't she trust Anaisha enough to admit she knew it wasn't a rumour, that the twins *did* kill people? Did Anaisha hate Ben enough to let them do that? To put such a catastrophic set of events in motion, then live with what she'd done? And what would that say about her if she did? She'd sworn to uphold the law, not bend it when it suited her. Shaq, on the other hand, she'd often thought of someone killing him, but mainly she'd imagined him getting ill in prison and dying from an illness. Plenty of times she'd muttered to herself that if he could just die, her parents would rest easier. But that line of thinking was considered wrong.

An eye for an eye…

"I could handle knowing I'd instigated something like that," she said. "You have no idea of the thoughts that go through my head. And anyway, how the hell would we approach them about it? I mean, you can't just go up to a set of twins and say you want them to kill someone for you, can you?"

"Apparently, that's exactly what you do." Janine studied her and seemed to come to a decision. "Forget I said anything, all right? We'll go down the legal route. Like you said, pretend we never had this conversation."

Anaisha couldn't let this go. She wanted to know more so admitted to Janine about having thoughts of Shaq being killed. Janine didn't bat an eye.

Instead, she smiled. "It's natural. I went through something horrific when I was younger, and I spent an awful lot of time thinking up scenarios where my abusers were killed. Rather than do that in the long term, I chose to go into the force, the same as you did after your brother died. But I'd be a liar if I said those thoughts didn't stay with me for years and still crop up even now. The same will apply to you, I'm sure. But it's the cross we bear. We promised to serve, and that's what we do."

Maybe I got it wrong and she isn't a bent copper. Or did she just say that to throw me off?

"Are you going to call it in, then?" Anaisha picked up her cup to finish her tea, annoyed her hand shook—and that was from the realisation that maybe she had a proper ally here, someone who thought wicked things like she did. If she opened up more, exposed her true thoughts, would Janine do the same?

Janine stared at her. "Which call am I making? The one to the station or…?"

It fully hit Anaisha. "Fucking hell, you *know* The Brothers, don't you?"

"Only from when I've spoken to them regarding crimes—they always have bloody alibis, though. But I know someone who can get hold of them—and that stays between me and you, right?"

Anaisha nodded, but she wasn't swallowing that crap. "You're lying, but if that's the way you want to play it, fine."

Janine got up and put the cups in the sink. "I thought you didn't want that, though, external forces being brought into it."

"If Shaq and Ben were gone, it would solve so much." Anaisha couldn't believe she'd said that, to Janine of all people, someone she'd thought was an upstanding member of the police force who always seemed to do the right thing, never putting one foot wrong. Then again, Janine had planted the seed in her head, so she wasn't as morally straight as Anaisha had thought. Could you be a good copper and a bent one at the same time? It was something she'd asked herself on many an occasion. "Don't listen to me. I don't know what I'm saying."

"You do, you're just scared to take that step. So, considering how you're unsure, it's better not to walk down that avenue. You'd have to explain the state of your face to your team, and when Ben doesn't turn up at work for days on end, you might be a suspect. Shaq, though… That could be arranged. And let me just say again, if you tell anyone about this conversation, no matter how much I like you and your parents, I *will* save my own arse over yours, understand? I'll deny every fucking bit of it."

Anaisha didn't doubt that, and a horrible, sneaky little feeling crept into her. "You work for them, don't you."

"Not much, and that's the truth. I used to be full-time, though, and I'm still on hand for their new copper. And again, I'll deny that until I'm blue in the face."

Anaisha wasn't stupid. She put two and two together and knew she was right when she said, "Flint?"

"I'm not saying a word on that. But sometimes, the only way to get things done is by alternative means. It's ethically wrong, but it fucking works."

"I thought I saw him today. At the sting. But he had a beard and a tan so…"

Janine's expression wasn't giving anything away, but her words did. "I found out this evening that Amateur's been caught, and that's all you need to know—not the how. You'll go to work and you'll go through the motions, but you will never, *ever* tell anyone that Amateur's…that he won't be a problem anymore until it becomes clear to everyone else that he isn't."

Anaisha digested that, surprised, shocked, and sickened that she didn't feel much about it except relief. She should be up in arms, she should want Amateur to be apprehended by the team, but because of the ordeals she'd been through regarding Shaq and Ben, she found that so long as justice had been served in some way, it didn't matter how. Was she a bad person? Should she resign, find a different job? Because with those kinds of thoughts, she shouldn't be a police officer.

Should she?

"What did he look like?" she asked. "There was a man with a beard who seemed off."

Janine shrugged and came back to the table. She sat. "No idea. I'll find out tomorrow when I see his body."

He was going to be killed?

Janine held a hand up. "Don't say a word to me about that, all right? Just don't. People like him don't deserve to live. He lured girls to order. People paid him a million quid for each one. You'll hear about it soon enough, because someone at the station's going to get an anon tip-off. I'll have to attend the scene because it'll be murder, and I'll just happen to find everything I need to point the finger at him. His phone contains proof, an offshore bank account. But like I said, go to work as usual, pretend you're elated that he's been found dead. Whatever, just keep your trap shut."

"It's my day off tomorrow."

"Then continue as normal."

"Why are you trusting me with this?"

"Because we're friends, and friends share secrets, don't they?"

Anaisha's mind spun with the information, but she nodded. "I won't say a bloody word, and if Shaq and Ben happen to wind up the same way, I won't be complaining." She hadn't asked outright, hadn't given the word, but yet she had.

Janine nodded. "Good. Now let's concentrate on tonight. You should prepare yourself for a long one."

One thing at a time. Deal with Ben's abuse and think about Amateur and Shaq later down the line. And Janine working for the fucking twins.

Anaisha sighed. Who the hell had she become to want to hide all of this?

But she knew. She'd always known she wanted justice however it came.

Chapter Nineteen

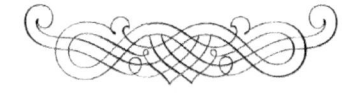

The forensic suit the twins had told Terry to put on rustled as he walked to wherever they led him. His hands sweated inside the rubber-type gloves, and his head itched beneath the hood, as did his face under the blindfold. He'd gone hot all of a sudden, knowing they were at the destination.

On the van ride over, George had filled him in on all the details. Who the man was and what he'd done. How he wouldn't confess to Summer unless more pressure was applied. George had only stabbed him in the dick, hadn't done much else to the wanker, so he needed more persuasion. Greg had explained that some men liked to retain control right until the end, so it wasn't unusual for the bloke to have admitted he'd chatted to other girls and not Summer. They got off on the power, but most of them broke eventually.

To find out it was Kendall Reynolds had come as a massive shock. He'd never have had him down as a pervert. A man who shagged about behind his wife's back, yes, but not a paedo. It had taken Terry a good five minutes to respond to that knowledge, and all he'd managed was a "Fuck." Terry had drunk pints with him down the pub, even as recently as when Summer had been speaking on London Teens, and all the while, that man must have known he'd been chatting to Terry's kid. What kind of sick bastard *was* he?

The blindfold came off, and Terry blinked in the harsh brightness of a strip light tube. It took a couple of seconds to realise what he was looking at. A naked Kendall hung from chains attached to the ceiling, and something was around his meat and two veg. Clingfilm? A patch of red in the region of his dick showed through.

Terry lifted his gaze to the man's face. He wanted to stare him in the eye, see behind the fucker's façade to the real man beneath—a deviant who'd changed the course of Summer's life, his and Willow's. Kendall had sentenced them to a kind of purgatory where they roamed around, lost, pretending to live, going through the motions but not enjoying a second of it.

Maybe after this they'd find specks of joy.

Kendall, a bruise on his face, stared back, the arrogant shit. Terry experienced a moment of pure hatred that swept up his body and brought on a cold sweat. A man who lured minors shouldn't have the audacity to glare at one of the parents like that, as if Terry were a piece of shit.

What if Kendall had nothing to do with Summer? Where was the proof?

No, he wouldn't entertain that. He trusted The Brothers. They wouldn't have strung him up if they weren't sure.

You're just having a little wobble again.

Which was understandable. Killing a man was a big thing.

He sensed the twins standing behind him. It bolstered his courage, their presence, and he silently thanked them for being there so he didn't have to do this alone. What if he stalled when it came down to actually hurting him, though? George and Greg could step in, take over, and Terry could watch, but he didn't want to lose face in front of the three men. He had to be strong.

He didn't feel as much anger as he'd thought he would. Maybe the shock of knowing who the perv was needed to be processed more. The fury might come if Kendall started talking, offering excuses or whatever. At the moment, he just resembled a modern-day Jesus, hanging, waiting for his execution, except there'd be no walking out of this cave resurrected. But there *would* be a celebration for him every Easter—a party to commemorate his death. There was no way Terry could put what he was about to do out of his mind and pretend it didn't happen so he could preserve his sanity. Every time chocolate eggs appeared on supermarket shelves, he'd be reminded.

And perhaps that was for the best. Maybe recalling it every year would keep Summer's memory alive, keep her vivid in his mind. He worried she'd fade one day, that the sound of her laugh would be forgotten. Time healed, so the saying went, but he panicked it would erase her.

He'd take the twins up on their offer. Go and see Vic. Talking to him would force Terry to open up about Summer, to bring her to life again. He and Willow could go together so they each knew how the other fared.

He felt better now he had a plan in place. A way forward after…after this.

"Why pick *my* daughter?" he asked.

That had bugged him from the start. Out of all the girls on London Teens, he'd chosen Summer. Her username must have caught his eye—Mermaid—as he was Fishy_For_Life, so there was a common theme going on. But was that all? There must have been something else.

"What was it about her, other than her name, that pulled you in?"

Kendall frowned. "I had nothing to do with her. You've got to believe me. These two think I asked her for photos and money, but I didn't, I fucking swear it."

"You *would* say that. *I'd* say that if I knew I was going to be killed. I'd do anything to get myself out of the shit."

"I've admitted to the others, because I did that, but I won't confess to something I didn't do."

"You're a wimp. I bet you'd say the same if the other parents stood in front of you. You'd lie through your teeth to them an' all. You're nothing but a coward, a yellow-bellied cunt." A spark of anger flared at last, and Terry lassoed it, roped that fucker in so he could nurture it, stoke it. "I can see it in your eyes. You're guilty as sin."

That was a lie. What he saw was fear and desperation, but that *would* be there, wouldn't it? When faced with the man who was going to end your life, you were bound to crap yourself, to want to plead your case. This was all a ploy, to get Terry to feel sorry for him. Control, like George had said.

"Why the fuck did you put those girls through what you did? Don't you care that they were frightened?"

"For money, plain and simple."

"Are any of them still alive?"

"A couple. Maybe three."

"Then do the right thing for once in your life and tell us where they were taken. The twins will go and get them, take them home, or the police can do it."

"I don't know where they are. I handed them over, and that was that."

"You don't give a shit, do you? You couldn't give a single fuck so long as you got paid. Is that all they were worth, a million quid each? A child is precious, and they're worth all the money in the world and more." The anger ignited. "Did you get off on looking at my daughter's photos? At her body that was too young for you to see?"

"I'm telling you, I didn't speak to her."

"What did you do with the pictures? Where are they?"

"I didn't *have* any pictures."

George stepped forward and punched Kendall in the face. "You're getting right on my hairy bollocks, mate. Stop fucking about and tell the man what he deserves to know. You took his kid away from him, the least you could do is put him out of his misery. Answer him. If you don't, I'll make this very fucking painful."

Kendall's bottom lip trembled, and he looked as if he wanted to cry. "All right, all right, I spoke to her. I fucked with her head because it was fun. I watched her when she left the envelopes, saw she was shitting herself, then I went home and wanked."

Oh God. Oh fuck. That was too much information. The thought had crossed Terry's mind before, that the man she'd given her nude pictures to had…had been pervy with them, but to actually have it said outright…

George passed Terry a knife.

Terry stared at it, his gloved hand shaking. He'd promised Willow he'd do this, and he wouldn't let her down, but he just needed a minute to process what would happen if things went wrong and he got caught for it. Prison wasn't ideal, but he'd suffer it for his daughter. The only thing bothering him now was Willow coping without him. She wouldn't, she'd made that clear when she'd said she couldn't live this shitty life on her own.

He glanced at George. "Swear to me this won't go tits up. Willow, I can't leave her to deal with any aftermath if I'm nicked."

"Janine will sort it. You'll be fine. He'll be washed before he's dumped, and you've got that gear on, so you have nothing to worry about. Just be careful when stabbing him. A lot of people cut themselves with the blade—their hand slips from the handle."

George stepped back.

Terry took a deep breath. "Do you know what you did to my daughter? How scared she was that her photos might be plastered all over social media? How she couldn't cope with the shame of what she'd let you persuade her to do so she killed herself? Do you have *any* conscience at all? And what about your wife, your little boy? They've got to live with your legacy, all the pointing fingers, people whispering behind their backs. They don't deserve all this, my missus doesn't, I don't, yet we're going to be left with the fallout of the choices you made. The parents of the other girls are going to find out exactly what happened to their kids, and their nightmare will begin all over again. Please tell me you at least feel a little bit bad."

Kendall sighed. "Sorry, but I don't, and that's the God's honest. The only thing I care about is that I'm not in Spain, sunning it up."

And that was it, the anger was unleashed. Terry rammed the knife into Kendall's stomach, twisting it, the fucker's face contorting in pain.

Kendall didn't cry out, so Terry withdrew the knife and stabbed and stabbed and stabbed until he did. The agonised groan that came out wasn't enough to assuage Terry's rage, and neither was the blood that spurted and dripped and coursed and pulsed and fountained. Terry slashed and sliced, walking around so he cut every part of him. Kendall drew his knees up with each kiss of blade on skin, and it jostled his body, the chains tinkling.

Back round the front, Terry took a moment to steady his ragged breathing. Blood had spattered his white suit, proof of what he'd done, proof he wished he could show Willow so she knew he'd honoured his promise and hadn't let George or Greg do it for him. He thought about Summer, how she might be looking down on him now, seeing the level he'd stooped to. She'd be sad. Shocked. But maybe she'd understand how much he loved her now. How far he was prepared to go.

Kendall wasn't dead. He breathed noisily, the air rasping in and out of him. Maybe even out of a ruptured lung, seeping through one of the stab slits. He released a weird noise, a strained gurgle, and his chin dropped to his chest.

It wouldn't be long now.

Terry wasn't proud of his actions. Not now he'd thought about Summer being sad. A part of him wished they'd informed the police, let them pick Kendall up so he could suffer in prison, but that was too good for him. Life was too good.

"I did the right thing," Terry whispered.

"Are you telling us or trying to convince yourself?" George asked.

Terry turned. "I don't know how to feel."

"Just be glad we stopped him from hurting anyone else. Think about that for now, and only that. You did a good thing. The rest, well, that can come later. Vic will help you process it."

Greg pushed himself off the wall where he'd been leaning. "It's not easy, killing. All right, *we* find it easy, but normal people don't. It'll take time to accept what you did. And if it wasn't you, it would have been us, so he'd have ended up dead anyway. That's one thing you can scrub off your guilt list."

"I don't feel guilty. I don't know what I feel, and that's the problem. The anger's gone, so what else is left?"

This empty feeling could be grief. He hadn't allowed himself to plunge headfirst into it, not fully, because he'd been hell-bent on finding Fishy. Now it was all over, what the fuck was he supposed to channel his thoughts on?

Willow.

He nodded to himself. Yes, she'd be his focus now.

Chapter Twenty

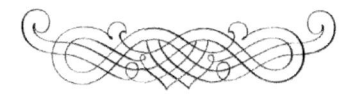

Anaisha was a ghost again in Dreamland, following Dayton down the pavement. It wasn't how it had been in real life. Shaq stood ahead, waiting with his long knife glinting in the light of a streetlamp, his legs planted wide, a maniacal grin splitting his evil face. The lads sat at the bus stop and shivered as she passed them. Had they sensed her? She ran ahead of

her brother, getting between him and Shaq, turning to push Dayton's chest, to force him back the way he'd come. He continued to walk as though she wasn't there, shunting her backwards, and she screamed at him to listen to her, see her. The knife slipped through her and into him, the pain of it sharp. She fell as Dayton fell, landing on top of him, his blood warm on her spectral belly. Panic seized her, and she cried, then she was sucked away from the scene.

She sat up in bed, the darkness crowding around her.

"For fuck's sake, not another one," Ben muttered beside her.

He used to be so good when she had nightmares, so understanding, holding her until the sobs subsided, but now her bad dreams irritated him, and he moaned a lot about having broken sleep. It seemed he picked fights for fun lately, any excuse to have a go at her. She wasn't in love with him enough to want to stay, to make it work, and she often thought about leaving him. But then he'd be nice again, confusing her, so she stayed, and life went on as usual, until the next time he got a cob on.

It seemed obvious, when he was in one of his moods, that she bugged him, she wasn't the right woman for him. And it was weird, every time she'd visited Shaq and came home to talk about it, he went quiet, no longer offering her words of support in how to get what she wanted out of him. Maybe her obsession with getting an apology was wearing thin with Ben. He used to have sympathy, but not these days. Now he said she was wasting her time and shouldn't go to the prison anymore because Shaq might tell her things she couldn't unhear, whatever that meant.

Her days had become a bit stormy. Maybe karma had done that thing where, because she'd gloated to Shaq that she had the life he wouldn't have for many years to come, she was being taught a lesson, forced to eat humble pie. Whatever it was, Ben had changed, and she didn't like who he'd become. Didn't like who she'd *become. Cringing inside at the thought of what he might do next or being afraid of him wasn't good—he knew that, she knew that, they'd been trained in domestic violence and how it affected the abused party—yet here they were, still together. Was she staying because she knew Shaq would taunt her if she told him she'd split with Ben? Maybe. It would remind her of the old days when he'd called her names in the street.*

She closed her eyes and again imagined him dying of cancer.

Better to do that than ponder her life.

She must have drifted off and jolted awake again, pressure on her throat. Blinking in the darkness, she stared at a shape above her — Ben, with a hand clamped around her throat.

"Shit, I can't do it. Fuck."

What did he mean?

He let her go and flopped over onto his side of the bed.

"What the fuck?" she whispered. "What can't you do?"

"Shut up and go back to sleep."

"No, I want to know what you were playing at."

"You wouldn't understand."

"Try me."

"Just be quiet. Seriously, don't say anything else."

"Why?"

"Because I might kill you and I don't want to."

Shock sent her bolt upright. "What the hell's **wrong** *with you?"*

"You don't want to know."

This was getting bad now. She had to get out, leave.

She left the bed and went downstairs. Made a cup of tea. Went through what had just happened. It wasn't right, and it had scared her, but with how Ben's moods had got worse recently, she'd have to play this carefully. Move out when there was no chance of him catching her.

For now, she'd bide her time and wait for the right moment.

Chapter Twenty-One

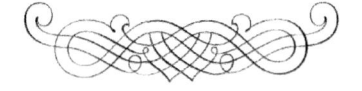

Anaisha had stayed at the police station until two a.m. Ben had been visited at the flat last night after he'd got back from wherever he'd stormed off to, then brought in for questioning, although a colleague had told Anaisha that he'd denied ever touching her. She'd expected that, so why had it hurt so much? Or maybe that was the wrong word. It had angered and frustrated her to the point of tears, and she'd repeated that she still wanted to press charges. Pointless, when one of his old work buddies headed her case, so inside her head she'd said: *Yes, the twins can take care of him now, because I've got a horrible feeling he's going to get away with this. He'll get a slap on the wrist, nothing more.*

Janine had been incensed that Ben's buddy wasn't taking this seriously. Anaisha had stayed over at her house, thankfully packing her belongings before they'd gone to the station. Janine now knew exactly what Anaisha wanted, and Ben would be dealt with. Anaisha didn't give a shit how the twins did it, she just wanted him punished, and if that meant him dying, good. He'd had the chance to admit what he'd done to her, and he'd squandered it. Now he could face the consequences.

She no longer cared that it would crush his mother. She no longer fully walked the straight blue line. She'd deviated, and would do so again when she returned to work tomorrow, something she'd insisted on doing despite her bruises. She'd fake it when she was told Amateur had been found dead, just as she'd fake it when Shaq was discovered in his cell, no longer breathing, and when Ben's body was discovered or he'd gone 'missing'.

This was the best way to move forward. Eradicate the scum.

She'd been through the prison checks and now waited at a table in the visiting hall. The chatter of other people coming to see their loved ones filled the room as a low mumble, as if speaking in an animated fashion wasn't allowed here, even though it was. She'd already bought herself and Shaq a coffee, plus a selection of baked goods—croissants, cupcakes, and two slices of Victoria sponge. She hadn't done that as a bribe to entice him to talk this time—his fate was sealed, and she'd get the apology she wanted via the person the twins would recruit to kill him. When that would happen she didn't know, and perhaps it was best she was unaware.

While she waited for Shaq to appear, she inspected who she was now—or rather, who she'd always been since her brother's murder. Before then, she'd never have agreed to what she had this morning. Janine had popped her head round the living room door on her way to work to announce she'd secured Anaisha a two-bed flat, admitting it belonged to The Brothers, although it was in a fake name on the tenancy agreement so Anaisha couldn't be held accountable for living in a place gangsters owned.

She didn't care that they owned it. The place was somewhere to lay her head at night and lick her ever-stinging wounds. Janine had handed her a set of keys and said she'd keep the other set so she could drop Anaisha's cases round there for her. She'd leave the keys on the worktop in the kitchen, plus the tenancy agreement. Although her parting words had been a little suspicious.

"You might not have to pay any rent if you play your cards right."

Anaisha had pondered that all the way here, and she was about to revisit it when the door at the back opened and an officer let the inmates in. She stiffened upon seeing Shaq—anger was never far away where he was concerned—and she schooled her features so he didn't know how much he still affected her. He'd get a kick out of knowing she wanted to wrap her hands around his throat and squeeze, so she wouldn't allow him that privilege.

He skulked over, acting as if he didn't give a shit whether she was there or not, but his eyes lighting up at the cakes and coffee betrayed him. He sat, slouching, clearly attempting to ignore the treats by looking around at everyone else, but greed and a lack of having many nice things got the better of him. He snatched up a slice of Victoria sponge—*what an animal*—and bit into it, jam oozing.

This was a dance, one they always did, but today she wasn't doing it. Sick of men controlling the narrative, she opened her mouth to ask him the same old question, but he held a finger up. Swallowed.

"Who hit you?" he asked.

"Ben."

"Your boyfriend."

"No, *ex*-boyfriend."

Shaq smiled. "So he wasn't lying to me, then."

She frowned, then caught up with what he'd implied—Ben had told him he was abusing her? How did they know each other? Had Ben contacted him after she'd told him who'd killed Dayton, or was it the other way around, Shaq writing to Ben once she'd gloated she had a fella?

She calmed down her need to shout at Shaq for answers and spoke calmly instead. Lied to him so she cut short any smugness he was feeling at having one over on her. "I had an idea you'd put him up to it. One minute he was nice as pie, then he changed. It didn't fit with who he'd been beforehand."

Did she feel sorry for Ben if he'd been coerced into harming her? No. He had the resources at hand to tell Shaq where to get off, even get his sentence extended with a bribery charge, but he hadn't.

Anaisha picked up a cupcake and peeled the paper casing away from one side. She took her time eating the whole thing because it would piss him off that she was being so casual and not barking at him for answers. Besides, her lip was sore with too much movement. "How much did you pay him to hurt me?"

"I didn't." Shaq smirked. He finished his cake and selected a croissant. "I had something on him."

"As in…?"

"He's a bent copper, did you know that?"

"Yes." Best she lied again. Ben could well be bent—look at Janine. But Anaisha wasn't sure if *Shaq* was lying. "So you blackmailed him."

"Something like that."

"How did you know where we lived?"

"I've got eyes on the outside. On you. Him. A few others."

My mum and dad? "I bet you have. Oh well, at least now I know it wasn't me he was actually railing against, he was forced into hitting me. It won't save him, though."

"What do you mean?"

"He laid into me last night, as you can see, and I've pressed charges. What you've told me will just add to the list of things he's done."

Maybe Edgar Nelly, who'd taken on the case, wouldn't be able to sweep this under the carpet now. Were Shaq's letters in the flat? Would Ben be so stupid as to keep them? She thought about his shifts this week—he'd be out all day. When she left here, she'd get hold of Janine. The twins might send someone to the flat to find letters.

"Hopefully he'll be sent here," Shaq said around a mouthful of pastry. "I could torment him even more, then. Never did like coppers."

For once, Anaisha didn't hate something Shaq had said, or the way he'd said it. She enjoyed the idea of Ben being stalked in here by this warped man. She didn't respond, though. Wouldn't give him any ammunition against her. For all she knew, he could tell a prison officer that she'd given him the go-ahead to bully Ben if he ever wound up in this nick, then she'd be questioned.

"Have you got an apology for me today?" she asked.

"Nope, and on no other day in the future either."

We'll see about that. "Fair enough. I gave you one last chance."

"What are you on about?" He swiped a cupcake off the paper plate and rammed the twirl of icing on the top in his mouth.

"God, you're paranoid." She smiled.

"I don't like that look you're giving me. Remember, I've got people watching you."

"And? Do you think that threat can hurt me after what you did to my brother? To my parents? They're just words. You can say whatever you like to me and it won't hit the spot. You've already done that by killing Dayton."

Yes, she'd let him know that was still raw, but he'd only have a while left to revel in it, and honestly, who *cared* what he felt. He was nothing to her but a savage bastard who didn't deserve to live. She wouldn't give him a title anymore—Dayton's Killer—and she wouldn't allow his imminent ghost to bother her, nor the actions of his past. Dayton was gone, there was no bringing him back, and Anaisha and her parents just had to accept that and try to live as best they could with that knowledge.

Time would never heal, but it would smooth over the rough edges so they were less prickly. In days, months, and years to come, they'd smile when thinking of him instead of crying. They'd celebrate the time he'd been here instead of the time he wasn't.

Shaq finished his cake. "Do you want to know the real reason why I chose Dayton?"

She braced herself for a barrage of words designed to upset her. "If you like."

"I was jealous of him."

"That doesn't fit with who you've told me you are."

"He didn't care he was mixed. He *liked* it. He knew who he was and got on with life. But me?"

"What about you?"

"I couldn't hack it. There was this bloke, nasty arsehole, and he reminded me every day for years that I wasn't whole. He called himself my teacher."

She held back a frown. Kept her expression neutral. How come he was opening up today? Why was he finally giving her an insight?

"I thought you *were* whole," she said. "That's what you kept spouting to Dayton and anyone else who'd listen. That was the point of you killing him, wasn't it, because you were 'whole' and he wasn't? Pure, I think you said you were."

"Except I'm not. I'm the same as you and him."

She hid her shock. Okay, Shaq wasn't as light-skinned as Anaisha and Dayton, he was pretty dark, but that didn't mean he was 'pure'. There were plenty of people who passed as what he called 'full'. God, she hated the terms he used.

"Your mum's white?" she asked.

"Yeah. She loves the man who put all this in my head. I can't tell her who he is because he said he'd kill me and my dad. I can't let him. I did whatever he wanted so he'd leave them alone."

"You should have told your parents, they'd have got you away from him."

"Nah, it was better to do what he said."

"So you wanted people to think both your parents are black so you didn't feel however he made you feel? You killed my brother, for what?"

"For being proud of who he was. For being allowed to exist without shame. It got me." He tapped his chest. "Got me right in here. It wasn't fair."

"What wasn't fair," she seethed, "was that you took it upon yourself to take Dayton away from us. What wasn't fair was taunting him for yonks beforehand. You became the teacher you hated, you know that, right? You *are* that man."

He sucked his teeth. "Nah, I'm not him."

"You are. Why do you even allow me to visit? What's the point in it?"

"Because you're the same as your bro, innit. You're comfortable in your skin, and I wanted to learn from you how to be the same. But I can't do it. He got into my head too much." He punched his temple, gaining a look from a watching officer. "What he said won't go away—it's still there sometimes."

She stood. "I won't be coming here again. Feel free to drink my coffee as well as yours."

She walked to the exit, going through all the checks until she stood out in the sunshine. Tears stinging, she took her phone from her bag and rang Janine.

"Ben hit me for Shaq."

"You what? Please tell me you're joking, because that's just sick."

"I wish I was, but it makes sense now. Ben was nice, then he wasn't. Regardless, he still needs to pay. How the fuck could he think it was okay to listen to Shaq of all people?"

"God knows."

"There might be letters in the flat, ones Shaq sent him. Could someone go in and get them, give them to me, and I'll hand them in as evidence?"

"Not to Mr Nelly, you won't. I'll give them to him so I can make sure he doesn't accidentally *lose* them. I'll make out you gave them to me; I'll ring George and tell him to meet me somewhere so he can pass them to me once they've found them. I'll photocopy them an' all so we have a set, log them in the system myself. Providing Ben actually kept them."

"I can't see him being that dumb, but then again, I wouldn't have thought he'd hit me for the man who murdered my brother either, but here we are. Oh, and can you ask them to get my electric toothbrush? I forgot to pack it."

"Yep."

"Thanks." Anaisha's mind wandered back to the previous topic. "He's bent, apparently."

"*Ben?*"

"So Shaq says. He's got something on him."

"Did you ever suspect he wasn't on the level?"

"No, but I didn't suspect you weren't, so maybe my bullshit radar isn't working as well as it should. Or you, Ben, and Flint are just too good at hiding who you really are."

"Who you've also become," Janine reminded her. "You crossed a line when you asked for the twins' help. There's no going back."

"I know. I don't want to."

It made her the same as Shaq in a way, the pair of them turning into people they hadn't thought they'd be, outside influences shaping them. She hated herself for understanding his reasoning, why he'd killed Dayton, what had driven him down that path. Everyone had a choice at that three-pronged fork in the road. Whether you went left, right, or continued straight ahead determined your future and that of others. The ripple effect was real.

"Shaq said someone called 'the teacher' influenced his thinking," Anaisha said. "I'll explain it all later. But if it wasn't for him turning Shaq's mind, Dayton would still be here."

"Who's the teacher?"

"I don't know. But we might be able to find out."

"Are you asking, but not asking, for what I think you're asking, regarding this teacher?"

"I think I am."

"Leave it with me."

Anaisha said her goodbyes and got in her car.

Then she let the tears fall and the sobs destroy her.

Who the hell had she become?

Chapter Twenty-Two

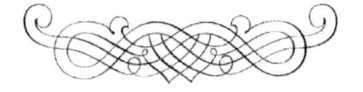

Ben had fumed all day. He hadn't had much sleep owing to Anaisha's stupid stunt. Because of the charges levelled against him, he'd been suspended until further notice, so he'd spent the morning catching up on kip and the afternoon and evening in the Royal Oak getting steadily plastered, mulling over the mistakes he'd made. Not only in hitting Anaisha but his other antics, too. He wasn't the most honest of coppers and regretted that now.

How had Shaq found out, though? Ben hadn't sensed anyone watching him during the times he'd spoken to crims off the record. He'd *never* felt as if he was under surveillance, yet he must have been.

He should never have gone to town on Anaisha, should never have obeyed Shaq's ridiculous commands in the first place. Then again, it had worked to keep Shaq off his back to begin with, the bruise resulting from a slap enough to appease the murdering little bastard in the form of a photo. Shaq had a mobile phone, something he'd managed to convey in one of his letters without outright saying it.

Did you know there are devices as small as a thumb that
can show you pictures?

Ben had sent images of a sleeping Anaisha to the phone number also disguised in the text. How the officers at the prison who read outgoing mail hadn't spotted it was anyone's guess, or maybe they didn't care *what* was written.

O, seventh heaven! There are twelve eggs to a dozen and six for half.
Did you know that a man once videoed a murmuration of starlings, slowed their collective flight right down, and counted one thousand, six hundred and seventy-two birds?

The digits in the whole paragraph made up Shaq's number: 07121261672. It had taken quite a few letters dropping onto the doormat for Ben to get the gist, though, and it wasn't until Shaq had written paragraphs in each containing the same numbers and the word 'dozen' that Ben had properly twigged.

He should have told a colleague, but the other words had stopped him.

Did you know, people who take cash for information and turn the other way when certain crimes are committed are considered unfit for the duty they're employed to perform? I wonder how quickly those people would find themselves without a way to pay the rent if someone were to pick up a thumb-sized device and speak into it? The tattler would get pleasure from knowing they'd ruined someone's day. Their life.

If anyone ever said "Did you know…?" to him again, Ben would lose his shit.

It was so clear what would happen if he didn't do as he was told, and at first it had been fine. The odd slap here and there, him goading Anaisha by being belligerent and causing arguments so he could hit her. He'd done the same to his ex-wife, vowing never to hurt another woman after that, but that had gone to shit. Last night he'd taken it a step too far. The pressure from work, plus the pressure from Shaq, had finally got the better of him. He hadn't been able to stop himself until it was too late.

He glanced around the pub. People surrounding him got on with their lives, likely with far less crap on their mind than him. He envied them their obliviousness, wished he'd gone down a different path so he could be like them. Wished he'd visited Shaq and warned him off—*paid* him off. Basically begged him to leave him alone.

This lot in here, drinking and laughing, roaring at the football on the telly, didn't know how lucky they were. Snooker balls clacked against one another, and it sounded so loud Ben wanted to scream. Panic built, that feeling of being out of control so intense he struggled not to punch the bloke next to him who ate his crisps too loudly.

He'd had enough. He left the pub just before last orders, the need to get home paramount. Edgar Nelly was confident he'd be able to make all of this go away, but Ben wasn't so sure. Anaisha had crowed that Ben was an abusive bastard, and she had Janine Sheldon on her side, of all people. Janine wasn't someone who'd back down when it came to a man hitting a woman. He didn't think he stood a chance, but if he got rid of the letters, there'd be no proof he'd hit her. It would be her word against his unless Shaq admitted to blackmailing him. During his interview, Ben had gone down the route that he hadn't touched her and she'd hurt herself in front of him, she was a nutter, whacking her face against the doorjamb and the wall, punching herself, wrenching her hair out.

What an utter wanker.

He walked briskly, leaving his SUV at the pub in the car park round the back; he'd had too much to drink. He entered the flat, for a moment puzzled as to why Anaisha wasn't there, then he remembered she'd moved out. Coming home from the station during the night and her not being here had thrown him for a loop, too, which was bloody stupid, considering. For some reason, despite her pressing charges, he'd expected her to still go home.

What kind of egotistical bastard are you?

He ignored that spiteful voice and went into the living room, flicking on the light. He paused. Sensed something was off. The place was as clean and tidy as ever, but the air felt…what? Different. It had that weird buzz to it when danger was close, as if static electricity crackled nearby or someone lurked, watching him. He checked the rest of the flat, and, finding nothing amiss, put the oddness down to paranoia. After all, why would anyone other than Anaisha have come in here? Her father wasn't a fighting man, and Ben doubted he'd turn up to dish out any just deserts.

The sad thing was, Anaisha didn't deserve what Ben had done to her. She'd been a good girlfriend, one of the nicest he'd had since his divorce, and a far cry from his ex-wife. And he liked her parents, especially her dad. They'd welcomed him into their family, not once bringing up the fact he was much older than their daughter and he'd been married before. They just wanted her to be happy.

Shame he'd never see them again unless this bollocks went to court, which it likely would if he didn't admit to what he'd done. If the prosecution contacted his ex for a character reference, he was fucked. She had plenty of stories she could tell the jury, and they'd have him banged up in no time. With him going into the dock, she'd finally open her mouth and spill the lot. She'd have no reason to be afraid of him then.

He ended up in the kitchen, crouching in front of the sideboard in the dining area. In the right-hand cupboard were his files containing documents—the tenancy agreement, his birth certificate, all that. He kept it locked, hid the key so Anaisha couldn't nose, and reached beneath the sideboard for it now. Pulled it out and twisted it in the lock.

He grabbed the blue folder and opened the flap.

The letters weren't there.

He snatched at the other folders, checking through all of them.

Nothing.

The key had been exactly where he'd left it, but that didn't mean anything. Whoever had nicked the letters would have had the sense to put it back where they'd found it. A horrible thought came to mind. Was Shaq playing him and Anaisha off against each other? When she'd visited him today, had he told her he'd sent letters to Ben and she'd looked for them?

He tried to recall when he'd last opened the folder. A month ago when he'd put the most recent correspondence away?

He stuffed the folders on the shelf and locked the door. Put the key back underneath—which was stupid because he lived alone now, so there was no need to hide fuck all. He rushed round the flat again in search of the letters, throwing open wardrobes and drawers. Anaisha might have stashed them.

Or taken them with her.

Fuck. Fuck!

His phone ringing in his pocket startled the shit out of him, and he took it out and stared at the screen. Jesus, what did *he* want?

Ben answered. "All right, mate?"

"Err, bit of a problem." Nelly sounded apprehensive.

"What with?"

"Um, you've basically been busted."

"Eh?"

"It would have been nice if you'd given me the heads-up."

Ben's heart thudded. "What are you on about?"

"I'm doing overtime, sitting here staring at letters addressed to you from a Shaq Yarsly. I've only just got round to having a gander. It's not looking good for you, pal."

"Oh, fucking *hell*!"

"I take it you're aware of their existence."

"Of course I bloody well am. Who brought them in? Anaisha?"

"No, Janine, but Anaisha gave them to her. She found them this morning when she nipped back to your flat. She'd forgotten her toothbrush, apparently."

She had, Ben remembered seeing it on the sink before he'd gone to the pub, but… "Hang on. She left her keys behind on the worktop, so how did she get back in?"

"No idea. Did she have a spare one cut? Technically, she moved out then entered the premises without permission, but I'd advise you not to split hairs. I can't make these letters go away, I'm afraid. Janine has copies and had already uploaded them to the file before she gave them to me, the clever little bitch. She clearly knows I was going to try and get you off, but that's not likely now, is it? Why the *fuck* did you keep them?"

"I don't *know*!"

"You're dumb as a bag of rocks, mate. Christ. Let me sleep on this. We could go with the angle that he's blackmailed you."

"But that doesn't solve the fact he's basically called me a bent copper! That will be looked into."

"Hmm, but we can say he's grasping at straws, he made that up. There's no proof of any wrongdoing on your part—is there?"

"Not that I'm aware of, unless the crims I've bribed step forward and drop me in the shit."

"Jesus. I'll ring you tomorrow, all right?"

The line went silent, and Ben stared at his phone.

"What the shitting fuck?" He threw it at the wall. It created a dent, a slither of plaster coming loose. The mobile fell to the floor, spiderweb cracks all over the screen. He stormed into the hallway—he needed to go on a proper bender, get so shit-faced he couldn't see straight. The Roxy was open for a while yet.

A shadow behind the patterned glass in the front door stopped him from going any further. The sound of a key entering the lock had him relaxing. Anaisha *must* have got a copy made and come back. Maybe they could talk, he could explain what he'd done, that he was scared of losing his job if Shaq told the police he was a dodgy copper. She was a good sort, she'd understand; he'd convince her to see things his way.

The door opened, and he was about to smile and beg for her forgiveness when he registered it wasn't Anaisha. Two men in forensic suits stood outside, hoods up, mouth masks in place. He racked his brain to work out if he knew them, but just having their eyes on show gave him fuck all of a visual. Why were they here? Why hadn't Nelly warned him SOCO were coming? Some friend he was.

One of them stepped forward, bringing a gun round from where his hand had been hidden behind his back. He pointed it at Ben, jerking it as if to tell him to go into the living room. Not SOCO then. Ben couldn't get past them, and there wasn't a back door, so he obeyed, scrabbling for something to say to make them go away. He stood by the window, cursing the fact the curtains were shut—none of his neighbours would see what was going on and help him. He slid his hand in his pocket, expecting to grab his phone, then remembered he'd lobbed it in the kitchen.

He stared as the man mountains came towards him.

"You need to come with us," one of them said.

The other nodded. "Hmm. Someone's been a very naughty boy, haven't they, sunshine?"

Chapter Twenty-Three

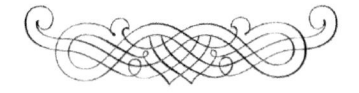

Shaq often wondered whether Ben would cave and tell someone what was going on. Controlling him from the inside was a massive thrill, despite it being the teacher's idea to drag the bloke into this. Shaq looked forward to the visits from his homeboy, the one who'd been spying on Ben, Anaisha, and her parents. The idea for that had come to the teacher after Shaq had

told him Anaisha had bragged about her happy life and that he couldn't have the same. Teacher wanted to ruin it for her, show her 'mixed-heritage arse' her life could go to shit again whenever he wanted. She'd already had so much good in her life compared to him, and it wasn't fair that she had some more. He'd left it for a long while before actioning the teacher's plan. Let her think she was safe in her relationship. Give her a false sense of security. Then he'd written the letters, getting ignored for quite some time until a response had arrived.

He wanted to learn from Anaisha, to be a better person, but the teacher wanted him to punish her. The teacher's words popped into his head from time to time, and it angered him because for long patches they remained silent and he thought he'd mastered blocking them out. When they appeared again, he cried on his bunk facing the wall, hoping his cellmate didn't hear him.

The little boy he used to be before the teacher had twisted his mind wanted his mother, wanted to feel safe, to have not killed Dayton, but the monster he'd become still had a hold on him, it seemed, especially after those visits, the ones that almost broke him. He didn't have to allow the teacher to come here, yet he did. He couldn't afford to refuse.

Shaq entered the visiting hall and spotted him straight away. Jesus, that smug smirk churned his stomach, reminding him of his childhood and how that smirk was sent his way during family gatherings, no one else seeming to notice them. Shaq approached the table and sat—no coffee or cakes like with Anaisha or Mum, but the teacher had a cup of something, likely tea. Selfish prick.

"Your mum asked me to send you her love."

Shaq stared at Uncle Dave, Mum's brother, and not for the first time wondered how Dave had managed to keep his feelings about Dad and Shaq away from his sister. Whenever he'd come round the house, he'd made out to her he was okay with who she'd married, but once he'd told Shaq his true feelings, the dark glances he sometimes threw Dad's way when he thought no one was looking had made sense.

"Right," Shaq said. "Still going round there to see her, then."

"Of course. Got to make sure my sis is all right."

"What, you think Dad's going to miraculously change after all these years? He adores her, you know that."

"His sort hide what they're really thinking. Savages, the lot of them."

Shaq shouldn't have expected any different. The names his uncle called black people were revolting, so wrong, and he'd called Shaq them too many times to count. How odd, that Shaq had been hurt by them yet had no trouble spouting them at Dayton and anyone else who fitted the bill, hurting them, too. Uncle Dave had infiltrated his mind so much that Shaq had become an awful piece-of-shit motherfucker.

"Did you do what I said?" Dave asked.

Shaq knew what he'd meant but played dumb just to annoy him, the only control he had over the wanker. But he had to be careful. If he pissed him off too much, the threats regarding Dad would start, and maybe he'd finally act them out.

"What are you on about?"

"Have you been bullying that bastard over there?" *Dave jerked his head towards Zebedee, a big black bloke originally from Ghana.*

"I've muttered a few things, yeah." *Shaq hadn't, he wouldn't dare, but he had to appease Dave.*

"Good. What was the outcome?"

"He doesn't know it's me. I've been saying shit in a crowd so he doesn't twig who it is. If he does, I'll likely end up dead, but I thought it would be funny to mess with him like that. He's been staring at everyone, trying to work out who's saying shit."

Dave laughed. "You need to get the whispers going, get other people in here on our side."

Strange, that Dave was using him to do his dirty work, spreading the word, saying it was "our" side, yet he despised Shaq for the colour of his skin.

It fucked with Shaq's head.

"Yeah, okay."

"If you don't, you know what'll happen."

"Yep, you'll kill Dad."

"Got it in one."

Dave guffed on about how Shaq could start a revolution, create discord amongst the prisoners, all with a few well-chosen words. Shaq had no intention of doing it, he didn't want to die in here, and keeping his head down had been the order of the day from the moment he'd stepped foot inside the place. But he'd pretend to pander to this bloke, tell him made-up stories of the stuff he instigated in here, and it would keep Dave happy.

His uncle rose and nodded as a goodbye, then left the hall. Shaq's homeboy came in then, and he went to the serving hatch and bought a couple of coffees and some doughnuts. At the table, he dished the stuff out then took the tray back.

Shaq had split his visiting hour into two slots so he could accommodate the pair of them. Dave hadn't stayed long, so Shaq would get more time with Richie, an extra fifteen minutes.

Richie sat. "Update. She doesn't look happy."

Shaq didn't need to know who he referred to. Anaisha. "Good. What about him?"

"He's jumpy."

"Prick."

"She visited Dayton's grave the other day. Sat on the bench and told him about Ben and that he's started hitting her. She was crying."

"Yet she makes out she's a hard cow in front of me now, so different to how she was in the beginning. Nice to know I can still get to her." There he went, acting a tosser, just because he'd come into contact with Dave again. It had to stop. "I need you to do something for me. I can't pay you, obviously, but if you can create a little accident, it'd be appreciated."

"Her or him?"

"Neither. I'm on about Dave."

"Oh, fuck me, your uncle?"

"Yeah."

"I'll sort it, no questions asked."

"Thanks."

Richie likely didn't understand why, seeing as he thought Shaq looked up to Dave, but Richie looked up to Shaq, and he'd do anything for him. Shaq had done to Richie what Dave had done to Shaq, infecting his mind—the circle of abuse, as it were. It had to end, and so long as Dave wasn't around, his mum and dad wouldn't get hurt.

"Mind you don't get caught," Shaq warned.

"It's okay if I do. I'll end up in here with you. I miss you on the outside, innit, bro."

Shaq smiled, although he now felt bad for manipulating Richie's mind over the years. But he wanted out of here, to become a reformed character, and he'd even agreed to some more therapy. If he could get Dave's words out of his head and prove he wasn't a danger to anyone of mixed race heritage, he could have that life he wanted, a wife and kids, a new start.

He doubted he'd ever stop picking on Anaisha when she visited, though, and he didn't know why.

Maybe he was evil deep down and Dave had just brought it out in him.

Mum had been crying, her red-rimmed, swollen eyes proved that. Shaq had spoken to Richie on the phone last night and knew damn well why, the coded message hilarious: "The duck doesn't quack anymore." Nothing else needed to be said on the subject, and with his calls probably being listened to, it was best no real details had been shared. Richie had gone on to talk about football and other things, just in case.

But now, Shaq would have to pretend to be shocked, upset.

"What's the matter?" *he asked.*

"I've got some horrible news."

"Is Dad okay?"

"Yes, he's fine. It's Uncle Dave."

"What happened?"

"Someone shot him in the back of the head on his way home from the pub. In the playing field next to the park."

"Shit. Why?"

"Random shooting, apparently, likely mistaken identity. It had to be, you know how nice Dave is. Wouldn't hurt a fly."

Shaq wanted to burst her bubble, tell her exactly who her brother had been, but it was bad enough that he'd hurt her by getting the wanker killed. But better that Dave was dead than Dad. He didn't reckon she'd get over losing her husband.

"Sorry," *he said.* "For your loss."

"It's yours, too."

"Yeah."

It wasn't.

"There was no CCTV, so no clue as to who did it," Mum said.

"The police will find out eventually."

Shaq doubted that if it was the playing field he thought it was. Richie didn't live far away from it and would have slipped down the alley at the rear of his street and gone indoors via the back garden. His mum was on sleeping pills so wouldn't have heard him coming home, and the neighbours either side weren't anyone to worry about. As they dealt drugs, they'd hardly be likely to phone the police and bring attention to themselves.

"I hope so." Mum sniffled. "God, I can't believe he's gone."

Did she feel like Anaisha, lost now her brother was dead? Shaq was responsible for ensuring two women had lost their siblings, for different reasons, and Mum would be horrified if she knew he'd had a hand in Dave being shot.

"When's the funeral?" he asked.

"Not sure yet. The police will be hanging on to his bo…body for a bit while they're investigating."

"They won't let me out to come. I'd only be allowed to yours or Dad's."

"I know."

Mum picked at a cupcake. He hated that he'd devastated her, but for his own sanity, and hers, he'd once again made a nasty decision. And it had been for the best.

That's what he told himself anyway.

Chapter Twenty-Four

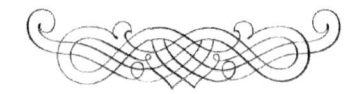

In protective clothing at just gone six a.m., Janine stood with Flint beside Kendall's body in the garage. Flint had received the tip-off, and he'd come out alone to see if it was a hoax, then phoned it in upon discovering the naked corpse—which was in a right fucking state. It seemed every part of the body on show had a stab wound, some of them crisscrossing over others. Terry had been frenzied, and who could blame him? Her job here was easy—this was clearly murder. No one in their right mind would be able to claim this as anything but a killing, and Jim, the pathologist, would say the same when he arrived, she was sure. It wouldn't take a post-mortem to establish that as a fact—no one could inflict these sorts of wounds on themselves prior to taking their own life.

"What's with the slice in his dick?" Flint whispered from the side of his mouth.

"Think about it," she whispered back. "He was involved in sex crimes—there's no way he didn't know the fate of those girls after he'd sold them. His dick's been stabbed as a way to get the point across to the police that he's a perv."

"His killer really went to town, had a lot of anger."

"Wouldn't you if your daughter was involved with this man?"

"So it was Terry? G and G think this bloke lured Summer?"

She was pissed off he'd mentioned Terry's name and G and G. "Don't you?"

"Of course I do, it's just when I gave them my thoughts on it yesterday, I wasn't there for the final confession. I was sent away. Any news on how Terry is?"

"No, and I haven't asked, but I'll know soon enough—and stop dropping names, for fuck's sake!" Janine glanced over her shoulder to check they were still alone. "I'll go and see him. He'll be top of the suspect list unless he's got a bloody good alibi."

At the sound of bootied footsteps scuffing the ground, Janine checked behind them again. The lead SOCO, Sheila Sutton, waited to enter the garage. Janine was glad Flint had been the one to check this out—Sheila had a bee in her bonnet about the so-called vigilante, aka The Brothers, leaving bodies and Janine always getting the tip-offs.

Janine had been a nervous stress-head as soon as the call had come in for her to attend the scene. She hadn't wanted any more of this shite on her plate, a twins-induced issue for her to deal with, but she'd be away from it soon enough. A baby didn't cook in the womb forever, and she'd be off on maternity leave, someone else taking over her role as team leader until she went back.

If she ever did.

She'd had a conversation with Cameron last night about her future and how he felt about the mother of his child doing something else with her life other than chasing criminals. The chat she'd had with Anaisha on the park bench, and watching that woman there with her children, had given her pause for thought. What if she *was* a good mother? What if that's all she wanted to be as soon as she set eyes on her child?

Flint's expression drew her out of her head.

"What?" she said.

"Nothing."

It seemed like he'd been on the verge of confessing something, or at least revealing his feelings on this case, how he was coping with knowing the facts before a body turned up and how he was handling that in front of their colleagues—and if he opened his mouth on that subject, she'd rip him a new one. It wasn't easy, she'd warned him it took time to get used to it, but now wasn't exactly the ideal opportunity to discuss it, especially with Sheila lurking and tutting every so often because they were taking so long.

"I need to talk to you," Janine whispered. "Somewhere more private."

Colin was off speaking to someone who owned one of the other garages, so she led Flint to the door where she removed her protective clothing and placed it in the designated bag. New shoe covers on, she stepped outside past Sheila and walked to the end garage, well out of earshot. For authenticity, Flint had entered the garage earlier with no protection on, so he strolled up to her without having to get undressed. Some techs, down on their knees, studied the ground outside Kendall's hideaway, and a photographer nipped in with Sheila to do his thing.

"What's the matter with you?" she asked. "You must *never* forget that listening ears are around, got it?"

"That's harder than I thought, plus having to keep shit straight in my head."

"Yeah, well, that's your life now."

"What did you need to speak to me about?"

"Anaisha's one of us," Janine said quietly.

Flint blinked. "Come again?"

"You heard me. I haven't told her outright what you do, but she guessed based on me admitting to being involved with the twins."

"Bloody hell, you had no right to include me in that. If you want to confess your bollocks, go ahead, but mine? No way."

"Think about it. With two of you, it'll make your life a damn sight easier."

"How do you know she's one of us and not some plant sent to trip us up?"

"Because she asked me, without actually asking me, to get the twins to kill Shaq Yarsly."

He reared his head back in shock. "The twat who killed her brother?"

"Yes, and she also wants Ben sorted."

"Her boyfriend?"

"Ex."

"What the fuck for?"

Janine frowned. "Haven't you heard the goss?"

"Clearly not…"

"Ben beat the shit out of her. She's pressed charges. And she's not long informed me that Shaq blackmailed him to do it."

Flint appeared nonplussed. "Why would Shaq want that to happen?"

"Beats me. To hurt her more than he already has? I don't know and I don't care. The pair of them are going to be offed, so that's two less scumbags on the planet, plus a third in the form of some bloke Shaq called his teacher, the one who turned his brain. The twins' PI can poke around regarding that."

"You need your head testing. You really do have a beef with some types, don't you."

"So would you if you'd been raped and abused in a basement flat. Those who intentionally hurt people need to pay the price."

His cheeks turned red.

She cocked her head. "What's with the blushing?"

"Nothing! It's fucking warm out, all right?" He gestured to the sun peeping from behind a white cloud. "Look, I'm sorry crap happened to you, and to Anaisha, but I'm not sure her coming into our gang—"

"I'm not in the gang anymore, not really."

"You are, you're doing their bidding right now and always will be as long as you're a copper."

"Hmm. Anyway, just in case you need an ally, or an alibi, you now know where to go. Anaisha. I'm not always going to be around, and like I told you before, me and you can't be seen as pally at work all of a sudden when we weren't before, so I can't cover your back. We'll get away with gassing today because of this scene. So, talk me through what happened so I don't fuck the story up."

"This is what I've been told to say: I received a phone call on my work phone—not unlikely because we hand out a lot of business cards. Someone, a man, said there was a body in the garage and that the dead man's phone had information on it that would implicate him in a crime—that he sells girls. Nothing was said about Summer Meeks, though, so you'll have to dig around about that or get hold of G and G yourself on that one. Oh, and there's a note, which I saw on the worktop in the little kitchen section."

"What did it say? I haven't had the chance to read it yet."

"That the deceased is Kendall Reynolds and he sold minors for money, approaching them on London Teens."

"There you go, then. London Teens being mentioned means I'll put two and two together regarding Summer Meeks and pass it on to the Internet Crimes team. Do you see how our mutual friends set everything up for me? For you? All we have to do is obstruct anyone who tries to derail the situation. Yes, that part is stressful, but that's what we get paid for."

"Plus there's a list of names on the note, Client 1, Client 2, right up to Client 10, and phone numbers beside them. Stands to reason what they are." He lowered his voice. "Are you going round to see Kendall's wife?"

"I'll have to, she's his next of kin. The twins will have prepped her on what to say, too. I'll need to go through the motions in finding out who the garage belongs to as well, crossing the Ts."

"I've already done that. I phoned in for a check when I found the body."

Relieved, she asked, "What else have you done?"

"I spotted a wallet beside the note which just so happens to have a driving licence and a Barclays debit card in it, both in Kendall's name."

"Did you touch it?"

He sighed, obviously annoyed she'd asked that. "No, I used a pen to flip it open. There's two transparent windows inside, and the licence and card were behind them. I *did* flop onto the sofa in shock at seeing the state of the body, though, if you catch my drift."

"Because you sat there yesterday?"

"Yes. I wanted to be sure, even though George told me earlier that a cleaning crew went through that garage like a dose of salts before the body was dumped, so that was the only thing I needed to have touched today; it disguises what I did yesterday. They also hosed him down with bleach. Oh, and the computer was restored to factory settings—they were going to keep it but decided to put it back on the desk."

"Nice of them to have told me," she said, sarcasm heavy. "I've been worrying about having to explain your DNA away so it sounds plausible."

"See? Too many cooks spoil the broth, and this is why Anaisha shouldn't be brought in on this kind of shit."

"That's the twins' call, I was just giving you a heads-up that she might become your little buddy."

"Thanks, I suppose."

"Lighten up, you crusty fucker. Right, sign out of the log and go and submit your statement at the station. Once I've passed on to Sheila about what's on Kendall's phone, I'll go and see his wife."

Flint nodded and hustled away, hands in his pockets. Janine stared after him, worried he wasn't up to this, that one day he might crack under the pressure. Still, not her problem.

She wandered towards Colin who'd left the man he'd been speaking to and approached her.

"What did he have to say?" she asked.

"Quite a bit regarding Kendall being here most evenings. The bloke"—Colin checked his notebook—"Robert Wannamaker, his name is, he uses his garage as a workshop. Carpentry and the like. So he's here a lot before and after his stint at the day job, doesn't leave until about eleven most nights. He's seen Kendall standing at his door a few times smoking a fag and using his phone, also going for a piss in the trees over there."

"Nice… Did he see anyone suspicious yesterday?"

"No, didn't see Kendall at all, but he stayed in his workshop all evening." Colin pointed to a Kia. "That car's Kendall's, though."

"Okay. I expect the wife will enlighten us more, or maybe she has no clue where her husband's been all those hours. I'll nip to let Sheila know what Flint told me, then we can go and do the death knock."

"What *did* Flint tell you?"

"We'll talk about it in the car."

Janine walked up to the garage door and peered inside. "Sheila, I won't come in because I'm not togged up, but just so you know, according to whoever phoned Flint, there's stuff on that phone regarding what the deceased got up to prior to death, so digi forensics will need to go through it. Likely the same with the computer, even though the caller said it had been restored to factory settings." She passed on what else the 'man' had said to Flint and that Flint had already peeped inside the wallet. "Oh, and he sat on the sofa when he found the body. The shock…"

"Thanks, I can rule any of his hairs or whatever out, then." Sheila stared at Kendall. "This isn't the same MO as our vigilante."

"I thought the same, despite there being a note, so Flint said."

Sheila glanced towards the back at the kitchen cabinets. "It's not the same—no sandwich bag, and the writing's different." She sniffed. "It stinks of bleach in here."

"I smell it, too."

"I reckon someone's cleaned it."

"Hmm. Right. I'm going to see the wife now with Colin."

Sheila sighed. "I feel for her, finding out what her husband was doing. Selling girls—selling anyone—is abhorrent. I'll never get over the depths humanity will go to when it comes to making cash. Why can't they just get a normal bloody job?"

"No idea. I'd better be off. Give Jim my best, and can you let him know I'll phone him later for his initial thoughts?"

"Will do."

Janine gave Kendall's body one last glance. *The fucking state of him…*

Then she left, hoping Ivory Reynolds was a good actress, because recently, Colin had been a little too perceptive for her liking. The last thing they all needed was him picking up on a vat of lies.

Chapter Twenty-Five

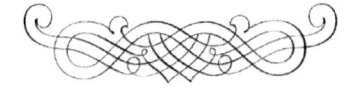

Ivory had expected officers in uniform, not this woman and a rotund man in casual clothing. She stood staring at them on her doorstep, their ID held aloft, her mind stuttering over the fact that this already hadn't gone the way she'd envisaged it in her head. If she wasn't careful, she'd give the game away, so she composed herself.

"Um, have I done something wrong?" she asked.

The woman, Janine Sheldon, smiled. It was a little sad, and Ivory supposed she dreaded having to break the news. All night, Ivory had imagined how Kendall had died, and now she might find out if they were allowed to divulge all the details. But did she even want to know?

No, best I don't.

Janine put her ID away. "Not that we're aware, no. Do you have a few minutes so we can come in and chat?"

Ivory nodded. "I've got to go to work soon, though."

She remembered what George had told her when the twins had dropped her home yesterday.

"Don't mention Marnie. If you're asked, pretend he never cheated on you, all right?"

"But what if she comes forward? You said you showed her a photo of Kendall."

"She won't. We'll pay her off. Threaten her."

She led the police into her kitchen where she could busy herself making tea. She'd not long boiled the kettle, having got up at seven, so it would only take a few seconds to reheat to a boil. "Do you want to sit down?"

"It's best if we do—if you do." Janine gave her that smile again and glanced at the kettle. "Colin will make us all a cuppa."

Colin, who didn't look too pleased about that, ambled over and opened a cupboard, presumably in search of cups. Ivory watched him, stuck in place, unsure whether she wanted him poking about or not. Then again, she'd have to get over that, because she suspected a warrant or something would have been issued so coppers could converge on this house, or maybe they didn't even need one seeing as Kendall was dead and the tenancy was in his name. She didn't know anything about that sort of thing and how it worked. Still, she had nothing to hide here, but whether Kendall did was another matter. If they found something, would they think she knew about it? That she'd covered for him?

Janine snapped Ivory out of her head by guiding her to the table and chairs by her elbow. Ivory sat, and Janine parked opposite. *This* Ivory had envisaged, the 'chat' she'd been fretting about.

"What's going on?" Normal people would say that, wouldn't they? People who didn't have things to hide. She hoped she'd successfully come across as suitably worried yet innocent.

"I'm going to preface the reason we're here with a few questions. What we've come to tell you is upsetting, and if it's okay with you, I'd like a few details first."

"Upsetting? What's happened? Oh God, is it Remy?"

"Who's that?"

"My son. He's round my mum's. He's poorly, and I've got to go to work, so she had him over last night to save me getting him out of bed this morning to take him there."

"No, it's not about him. When was the last time you saw your husband?"

Ivory found she couldn't actually recall. "My mind's gone blank. Hang on…" She remembered and passed on that detail. "Why?"

"So he didn't come home last night?"

"No."

"What about the night before?"

"I haven't got a clue because I wasn't here."

"Where were you?"

"At work. I clean at a women's refuge. There was a lot to do, and I finished late. I ended up staying over. Remy was with me."

"What's the refuge called?"

"Dolly's Haven."

"What did you do yesterday?"

"Me and Remy were at Haven. Like I said, he's not well, so he was with me."

"What about last night?"

"I dropped Remy off at Mum's then was here for a while. After that I went to the pub. I thought, seeing as Mum had him, I'd take a bit of time for myself."

George had suggested she go out, be seen during the time they'd planned to kill Kendall. She'd agreed, seeing no reason not to; they clearly did this sort of shit all the time and knew how things panned out. He'd told her to go to The Eagle because the owners would vouch for her without question, as would the old man called Stanley who she'd been told to speak to for most of the evening.

"Which one?" Janine asked.

"The Eagle, the one opposite the factory."

"How long were you there for?"

Ivory picked her phone up and accessed her Uber app to check. "A taxi picked me up here at six, then there was another at eleven. I came home and went to bed."

"Can anyone verify that you went to bed?"

"Not unless they were nosing out of their windows and saw me switch the lights off, no."

"Is it unusual for your husband not to come home and for you not to seem bothered about it?"

Ivory's cheeks heated—she hadn't expected an officer to be so rude but supposed it *would* look odd to outsiders that Kendall did as he pleased and she didn't mind. "He does his own thing, I do mine, so no."

"Where is he during those times?"

"I have no idea. Look, can you get to the point, please? You're worrying me."

"There was an anonymous tip-off that came in about a garage. I'm sorry to inform you that a body was found inside and, going by the identification in a wallet at the scene, we believe it to be your husband."

"What? A body? A garage? But Kendall hasn't *got* a garage!"

"Checks have been made, and he owns it. So you were unaware of it?"

"This is the first I've heard. And he's dead? How?"

"We're treating it as murder."

Ivory slapped a hand over her mouth. Colin brought the cups over and sat, and she got the distinct impression he studied her to see if her reaction was genuine or not. Or maybe she was just paranoid. Maybe she should be crying. She imagined losing Remy, and tears came easily. One slid down her cheek.

"Who the hell would *do* that to him?" she asked behind her hand, then lowered it to her lap. She entwined her fingers to stop them from shaking.

"We don't know," Janine said, "which is why we're here. We need as much information as possible to build up a picture of who he was."

"Did he suffer?" That would make her look like she cared.

"I'm afraid so."

"Oh God…"

"I'm sorry to distress you by asking another question, but did he have any enemies?"

"Not that I know of."

Janine pulled a cup across the table, blew on the tea, and sipped. "What was your marriage like?"

"I won't lie, we've grown apart a bit, hence us doing our own thing, but it's okay." Good, she'd remembered to speak in the present tense like George had instructed. "We kind of bumble along."

"What did he do for a living?"

"He's a brickie. Oh...could it have been someone from the building site who did it?"

"I don't think so. Information has come to light that Kendall was involved in something illegal involving children."

"No." Ivory shook her head. "No, no, he wouldn't do that."

"It's been suggested that he talked to girls on a site called London Teens, groomed them, then abducted them, sold them to buyers. Is that something you can imagine him doing?"

"What? No! I wouldn't be with him if I thought he was up to anything so disgusting. Are you sure you've got your facts right?"

"The investigation is ongoing. We'll discover more as it progresses. Do you know of a Summer Meeks?"

"Only from the news. That girl who was found in the park." Ivory placed a hand on her chest. "Oh no. He *didn't*…"

"We don't know, but we *will* find out." Janine drank more tea. "So you had no inkling of what he may have been up to?"

"Bloody hell, no. I can't… This is just horrible. His mum's going to be devastated." Ivory glanced at the clock. "Shit, I'm meant to be at work in half an hour. There's no way I can go in now. Can I just give my boss a quick ring?"

"Please do, and pass me the phone afterwards. I want to arrange to visit her to check you were at the refuge when you said you were."

"Why would I lie?"

"You'd be surprised what some wives are prepared to do for their husbands—and how many react by killing them when they find out what they've been up to."

Ivory had had enough. She slapped the table. "Don't you *dare* imply I had anything to do with those kids or that I killed him. What Kendall did was his own business, and I'd *never* condone him selling girls. I have a child of my own, for fuck's sake."

Colin raised his eyebrows, glanced at Janine, and gave her a filthy look.

Is he on my side? Oh God, this is harder than I thought. I'm going to fuck it up. I'm too scared to keep this up.

So she didn't have an even bigger wobble, she snatched her phone up and jabbed at the screen. "Sharon? It's me. Sorry, but I can't come into work today."

"So it's done?" Sharon whispered. "Good."

"Kendall's…he's been found dead, and I…"

"It's for the best, you know that. Take a few deep breaths. You've got this."

"Okay. The police want to talk to you. Hang on." She passed the phone across.

Janine took it and walked to the corner, speaking low.

Ivory glanced at Colin.

He now seemed to feel sorry for her. "It'll be all right, love."

She nodded, swiping at her tears of anger, brought on by Janine's accusations. "I can't…this is all too much. I had no clue…"

"Do you have someone you can go and sit with?" he asked. "Other officers are going to have to search this house, I'm afraid."

"I'll go round my mum's."

Janine put the phone on the table. "Do you need a lift?"

Ivory bristled. "I can walk. It's only round the corner."

Janine stared at Colin, unspoken words flying between them.

Colin rolled his eyes at her, gulped some tea, then stood. "I'll go and wait in the car, then."

Janine waited until he'd left. She stood in the kitchen doorway, staring through to the front door. Then she turned to Ivory. "You did well."

"Pardon?"

"Sorry I had to come down hard on you, but I have to look like I'm doing my job in front of him." Janine jerked her head towards the door. "I can't have anyone suspecting I work for the twins."

Ivory sagged with relief. "Why didn't they warn me someone on their books would be coming today?"

"So your reactions seem genuine. Think about it, if you knew I was on your side, you would have acted differently."

"So is that it? Will anyone else accuse me of knowing about those girls? Or say I killed my husband? For the record, I bloody didn't."

"No, someone else did, but he won't get in the shit for anything either. Now, I'll drop you round your mum's, ask her what time you turned up with your son yesterday so Colin thinks I'm doing my due diligence, and that will be it—or I hope it will be once I put it forward that I don't think you're a suspect. You'll have to give a formal statement, but I can come back and do that with you so we get everything straight, all right? Oh, and I'll need your keys to pass on to the forensic team."

Ivory stared at her. "I just want all this to go away."

Janine smiled. "And it will. I'll *make* it go away."

Chapter Twenty-Six

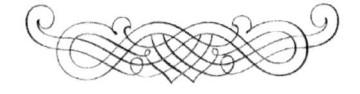

Terry had known this would happen, but it didn't make it any easier. He had to watch himself if he wanted to get through this without Colin picking up on something. Janine would steer her DS away from suspecting him—that was her job, and he imagined The Brothers wouldn't be too happy if she failed—but what if Colin got a bee in his bonnet about something and kept pushing? Would George give the order that the bloke should meet with an unfortunate accident?

Terry had lied in life before—didn't everyone?—but never as a murderer, and he was going to have to in order to keep himself out of the nick. He had so much to hide now, and if he could get through this interview without any mishaps, he'd call it a miracle.

His guts cramped, and nausea wreaked havoc. He swore the residue of his crime seeped from his pores in the guise of sweat, giving him away.

Willow sat beside him on their sofa. Janine and Colin perched on the armchairs either side of the fireplace looking right at home. Terry and Willow knew them both from when Janine had been called out to the scene the day Summer's body was discovered in the park. Of course, as it wasn't murder, someone else had taken over the case, but she'd let Terry know on the quiet that she worked for the twins and they'd do their best to find the scumbag Summer had been speaking to.

George had taken him through what he should say and how he should behave today. Terry and Willow had to step up on the stage and act in front of Colin who had no idea what Janine got up to behind the scenes.

We can do this. For Summer.

"Why are you here?" Terry asked.

"There's been a development in Summer's case," Janine said.

"Have you found the bastard, that Fishy cunt?" Terry asked, as bolshy as he always was with her, with everyone. Best he remain true to form. "And why are *you two* dealing with it anyway? Summer wasn't murdered."

"Because someone else was, and we have reason to believe the body is Fishy's. It was found early this morning."

Willow let out a shrill whimper and stuffed her fist between her teeth.

"Who is it?" Terry demanded. "His real name?"

"We'll get to that in a minute."

Janine glanced at Colin who nodded, raising his notebook in answer to her silent question. He was going to write things down, maybe put two and two together.

Fucking hell.

"You know I have to ask, so don't take offence," Janine continued. "You first, Terry. Where were you yesterday?"

"At work, then I went to the pub. The Angel, before you ask."

"How long were you there for?"

"I stayed until about midnight. Got a cab home."

"Did they have a lock-in or something?"

"Err, no. I was…" He shifted uncomfortably for effect, taking a quick glance at Willow as though ashamed, then giving Janine his focus. "I was…I mean… I went round the back, to the parlour."

"You did *what*?" Willow shrieked. "You let some woman touch you? A woman *like that*? Of all the things you've done, that's just the lowest. How *could* you?"

"It was for a massage, not any how's your father," he said. "My sciatica…"

"What sciatica?" Willow gave him a filthy look. "That's the first I've heard of it."

"We haven't exactly been having scintillating conversations lately, for obvious reasons, and I didn't want to worry you. We've lost our kid, and you've got enough on your plate without me mithering."

She glared at him. "Was it just a massage?"

Colin piped up. "Err, in Terry's defence, there's actually no proof anything else goes on in that parlour, just rumours."

Willow huffed. "Typical men, you all stick together."

Janine held a hand up. "Colin's right. There's no proof. People like to gossip, make more out of something than is really there." She smiled at Terry. "So you had a massage. How long were you in there for?"

"An hour. I was drinking at the bar before that."

"And you came straight home at midnight?"

"Yeah."

"He got home about ten past," Willow said, playing her part well—she sounded like she'd begrudged backing him up. "I heard the taxi door slam and got up to look out of the window."

She was bloody good at this bullshit lark, and it worried Terry. Had she acted in the past? Lied to him? If he didn't know she was pretending now, hiding something, he'd never have twigged.

"I got out of bed when he rolled in," Willow went on, "but had I known he'd been near one of those women…"

"Bloody hell, love, stop speaking about them as if they're shit under your shoe. They're qualified masseuses, that's it, nothing more. Whatever she did, it got rid of the pain going down the back of my leg, so she must know what she's doing."

Willow buttoned her lips, her cheeks turning red.

"And where were *you* yesterday?" Janine asked her.

"I pulled a double shift," Willow sniped. "Got home around eleven. I also got a taxi. Pete's Cabs, if you need to know."

"I'll have to check that—and the cab firm you used, Terry."

"Do whatever you have to," Willow said, "because Fishy's death is nothing to do with me, and Terry might be a gobby shite, but he hasn't got it in him to murder anyone."

"I'm just going through the motions," Janine said. "Of *course* we don't think either of you did it, but we have to establish alibis for the record. Okay, so…here comes the bit where you might know Fishy. Please remain calm if you do, all right? Getting lairy at us won't solve anything, we're just the messengers."

"Get on with it, for fuck's sake," Terry groused.

Janine inhaled. Let it out. "Do you know Kendall Reynolds?"

Terry scowled, and Willow gasped.

"Yeah," Terry said. "You're saying *he's* Fishy?" He recalled what George had coached him to say so it didn't look like he'd killed him. "Sorry, but I don't believe you. Kendall's a good bloke. I've played darts with him and shit down the pub, had a few bevvies. Nah, you're having us on."

"His wife..." Willow whispered. "Oh God, and her little boy... That poor woman."

"You know Ivory?" Janine asked Willow.

"Only to nod to down the shop. She's always been a bit distant. Doesn't seem to have any friends." Willow scrubbed a hand down her face. "Why the hell would Kendall want to speak to a teenager? He doesn't seem the type."

"This is the bit I haven't been looking forward to passing on."

Janine took another deep breath and explained about the anonymous allegation that Kendall kidnapped girls after speaking to them online then sold them to perverts.

"Jesus Christ!" Willow shot up and paced. "He could have done that to Summer. She could have been one of those girls—"

"Except she wasn't," Terry interrupted. "She killed herself before it got to that point. Maybe that's why she did it because she knew what was coming next."

Janine shook her head. "There was nothing on her laptop or in her Teen chats that can prove that. Maybe Kendall only toyed with some girls for his own enjoyment and the ones he procured for clients were the big paydays."

"Thank God Summer didn't have to go through that." Willow sank back onto the sofa. "I'm just…I'm just so *angry* he spoke to her at all, that she got tricked into thinking he was a lad. My baby…"

Terry put his arm around her. He struggled with the same thing himself. Their innocent Summer, duped like that. Coping with it all on her own. If only she'd opened up to them, they could have gone to the police. Then again, what good would that have done? They hadn't been able to establish who'd used the VPN access.

"What happens now?" he asked around the lump in his throat.

Janine sat forward. "The information found on his phone will be followed up, plus some phone numbers on a note left at the scene, and hopefully they'll lead to the buyers. If they were sensible, they'd have used burners to arrange the deals, but we might get lucky and catch them. We'll have to scour the missing persons database, see if we can work out which girls have been taken regarding this case. Just so you know, Ivory had no idea. She's heartbroken."

"I bet she is," Terry said. "She'll have a lot of people pointing fingers at her when this comes out. Some will think she knew."

"Unfortunately, yes." Janine stood. "We'll get your alibis checked out. I'm sorry you're going through this, but at least there's a resolution now. Knowing that man's dead is a small consolation, I realise that, but I hope it makes you both feel better. A life for a life, as it were, although pretend I didn't say that."

"I agree," Colin said. "Fucking bastard scum."

Terry remained where he was, leaving Janine and Colin to see themselves out. When the front door clicked shut, he peered out the front to make sure they'd really gone. They got in a car, and he looked at Willow.

"Fuck me, that was hard, pretending. Do you think I'm in the clear?" he asked.

She nodded. "Yes. You said George told you Janine would sort everything, so we just have to hope she does. I can't...I can't cope with you going to prison. I can't do this...this fucking *shit* life on my own."

That was the second time she'd said that to him.

He hugged her, kissing the top of her head. "You won't have to. I'm not going anywhere, love. It's you and me together now. Always."

Chapter Twenty-Seven

Despite the bruising and a sore lip that had now scabbed over, Anaisha had come into work just like she'd said she would. When she'd walked in, Oliver had muttered something about her needing more time off to recover, but she'd insisted on staying. Especially because news had come in that Kendall Reynolds was Amateur.

Oliver stood at the front of the room, deflated as he passed on the news. An hour had gone by with him going through the new information, and he was drawing to a close. "I wanted us to catch him, but someone else beat us to it. What's everyone's take on this? I mean, you can see the crime scene photos, he's a bloody mess. He didn't do that to himself."

Anaisha stared at the images on the whiteboard, held there by magnets that resembled big Smarties. The startling shots also filled the interactive board and seemed starker there, more real.

"Could it have been one of the clients you mentioned?" she asked. "What if, because Amateur wasn't able to pick me up at the Odeon, the customer got arsey with him? What if the man by the wall was a client?"

Oliver nodded. "It's a possibility. There's no definitive proof yet that the dead man is the one who spoke to Summer Meeks, but it's looking highly likely. We've basically got to hand all of our files over to Janine Sheldon. She and her team will deal with it now."

"What will we be doing next?" Anaisha reached for her cup of tea. "Will I be going back to response?"

"No, I got the confirmation for you to stay on this team. We'll move on to the next internet crime on the list. One case in particular has piqued my interest more than the others. Fraud. We're going to be setting up another sting. Before that, as you're all aware, there's a lot of groundwork to be getting on with. We need to integrate ourselves in the fraud, become a victim."

"What type of fraud is it?" Fay stretched her arms up and rotated her wrists.

"A life insurance company targeting the elderly. So, put Kendall out of your minds. It's done and out of our hands. Just be glad he was caught." Oliver used the clicker to swipe the death photos from the interactive, bringing up a bullet-point list. "Right, Life Cover Express…"

Anaisha tried to concentrate, but her mind was on Ben, Shaq, and the teacher, plus what she'd asked to be done. Then there was Nelly who hadn't contacted her about the letters, yet Janine had handed them in yesterday. He must be stalling, working out how he could get Ben out of the shit. Where was Ben today? The pub, probably. That was always his go-to place when he needed some space to think. He wasn't at work, she knew that much, because he'd been suspended while the investigation into her accusation took place.

She forced herself to listen to Oliver and what her role would be.

"As you were so good at speaking to Amateur—uh, Kendall—you can be the customer who wants life insurance, Anaisha. Now, you have to make out you're an old lady and new to this, talk to them on the chat function, so it'll be typing, not speaking. There's been previous complaints about a company called Lifetime Pensions where money has been paid in, then it disappears from the customers' accounts. The team investigating that have worked out Life Cover Express is the same people—or the same VPN anyway—so now it's our turn to have a bash at it. Are you up for that?"

Anaisha nodded.

"Good, then let's crack on."

Chapter Twenty-Eight

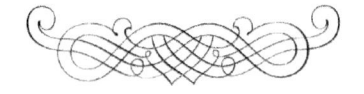

The morning had flown by, and Janine sat alone on the bench in the park with her Thermos full of decaffeinated tea in hand and an empty packet from a supermarket sandwich on her lap. She mulled things over. On paper, Ivory, Terry, and Willow weren't suspects—checking out their alibis had proved that—and Colin was convinced enough to stop banging on about it. She'd successfully persuaded him that Client 10 had killed Kendall, a suggestion Anaisha had made on the quiet.

News had come to light just before Janine had nipped out for lunch. Some information gleaned from Kendall's phone—messages he'd deleted but the forensic team had recovered—basically told the story of nine girls who'd been snatched and sold, then mention of a girl of black and white ethnic heritage. Going by the dates of the messages between Kendall and his customers, Janine's team now had a timeline they could follow, matching the dates the girls went missing to those on the missing persons database, and to the bodies that had already been found. Hopefully they could narrow it down so the parents could be informed that their daughters had been taken for a reason. A horrible reason and one Janine didn't want to impart to them, but it was her job, and she'd see this through to its conclusion, unless the investigation was still ongoing by the time she went on maternity leave.

There was a hell of a lot of work ahead, but it would keep her busy in between other murder cases that were bound to come her way.

She rose, stretched out the kinks in her muscles, and made her way back to the station. In the car park, she paused. Nelly stood talking to another officer. He waved his arms around then slapped a palm to his forehead, visibly shaken and very much giving the impression he was about to blow a gasket.

"What's happened?" she asked, curious as to whether Nelly was ranting to a sympathetic ear about the letters she'd handed to him.

Nelly rounded on her. "You'll be pleased to know Ben won't be a problem for Anaisha anymore."

"What?"

"He's fucking *dead*!"

The news didn't stun her, but she acted as if it did. The only thing that was a shock was that it had been done so soon. George clearly hadn't wanted to wait. "How? I mean…what the hell?"

"He was found in his car that was parked at the back of the Royal Oak. He blew his fucking head off. Where he got hold of a gun I don't sodding know. This is Anaisha's fault. If she'd kept her stupid little mouth shut—"

"Hang on a minute," the other officer said. "She had every right to press charges if he beat the shite out of her."

Janine smiled at him—Harry? Henry?—then addressed Nelly. "Guilt has a way of creeping up on people like Ben. Did you tell him about the letters by any chance?"

"Yeah. So?"

"Then he knew he was fucked, that he wouldn't get away with it. He topped himself rather than face any consequences. You'd be better off not sticking up for him. People will think you condone domestic violence. Has Anaisha been told?"

"I was just going to do that now."

"Don't bother, not with your attitude towards her. I'll get hold of her. The last thing she needs is you wading in with your size tens while you're in a shit state."

"Ah, fuck you." Nelly jabbed at the keypad by the door and disappeared inside.

Harry or Henry shook his head. "What the hell's wrong with *him*?"

"No idea." Janine smiled again and entered the station. She took her Thermos to her office, popped her sandwich packet in the bin, and shut the door. Burner phone out, she rang Anaisha. "Where are you?"

"At work."

"Are you sitting down?"

"Yes…"

"Watch how you react to me and what you say if you've got company."

"Right…"

"I told Nelly I'd ring you. It's done."

"Which one?"

"Ben."

"That was fast."

"I thought the same. I expect George thought it best to get rid of him sooner rather than later so it reduced any risk to you. Ben could have got fisty again, see."

"Do you know how it was done?"

"He shot himself in the head."

"Christ."

"The gun won't be traced back to them, trust me. I'd better get back to work. Nelly's bound to get hold of you anyway to let you know the DV case won't be going ahead. Act accordingly."

"I will."

"*No* wobbles, understand?"

"I get it."

"Good. Speak soon."

Chapter Twenty-Nine

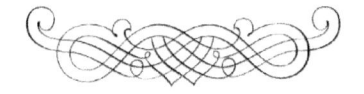

Shaq had eaten his lunch and now dipped plastic plates in the full-of-water sink before they went into the catering-sized dishwasher. He was lucky, being given this job. Everyone here wanted a stint in the kitchen because it was easier than all the other shit on offer. Only the most trusted were allowed near the knives (he wasn't one of them, for obvious reasons), and an officer stood guard at all times, watching whoever used them, ensuring none went missing. There was even a log to make sure they were all put back at the end of every cooking session. Shaq wasn't allowed to wash them, someone else did that.

The sink and dishwasher area was around the corner from the main kitchen, kind of secluded behind a half wall and perfect for Shaq. His job consisted of dipping and stacking the plates, then, when the pile was high enough, he moved along to the steel table beside the draining board and put the plates in the dishwasher racks. He then pushed those into the side of the machine, and they came out onto another table where someone else put them away. That someone, Fred, had not long gone off to the toilet, so the last rack that had been sent through just sat there.

"Fuck's sake. It's going to mess up my routine."

The hairs on the back of his neck rose, something that happened regularly in here—so much so he ignored it half the time, even though he shouldn't. Danger was never far away, but he'd kept below the radar so far and didn't piss anyone off. Getting shanked wasn't his idea of a good time, so he made himself invisible as much as possible. He replied when he was spoken to and kept his eyes averted.

He'd sort of said sorry to Anaisha yesterday, hadn't he? By explaining why he'd killed Dayton, the real reason, it was a form of apology. No way would he say the word outright, but at least he'd given her something. Therapy seemed to be working. Even a week ago he'd never have opened up to her like that, but something had clicked in his last session.

Uncle Dave being dead had worked wonders.

The feeling of someone standing behind him grew stronger, so he peered over his shoulder. Zebedee stared at Shaq, leaning on the edge of the wall that separated this part from the main kitchen. Fuck, had he found out what Dave had wanted Shaq to do to him? Shaq hadn't spoken more than half a dozen words to Zebedee, ever, so if it wasn't the Dave thing, why did he look so angry?

Zebedee spread two fingers and pointed at his own eyes, then turned his hand around to point them at Shaq.

I'm being watched? Why?

Shaq wanted to turn his back and get on with dipping the plates, but if he did that, Zebedee might come up behind him, catch him off guard. At the same time, Shaq couldn't keep gawping at the bloke or it'd look like *he* wanted to start something.

Fred bustled past Zebedee. "Sorry. Didn't mean to bump into you."

"Not a problem," Zebedee said.

Fred came over to the sink. The old man, in for murder with no chance of parole, had certainly taken his time in the toilet. Instead of emptying the rack, he stood there and guffed on about his new cellmate's snoring and that he'd spent most of the night imagining ways to kill him. Shaq smiled and nodded in all the right places, glancing at Zebedee who gave one final stare then walked off.

"Ah, he's gone," Fred said. "I saw you needed a bit of help which is why I was talking instead of working. What the fuck have you done to Zeb?"

"I can't think of anything." Shaq faced the sink and picked up a plate to dip it.

"I mean," Fred said from behind him, his mouth close to Shaq's ear, "you need to pay for what you did to that lad, don't you."

Shaq stiffened. "I'm paying for it by being in the nick."

"Yeah, but you haven't showed any remorse."

Something sharp pressed into Shaq's side, and he stiffened, shit-scared that he was in a situation he couldn't get out of, trapped as he was by Fred's body at his back, the lip of the sink in front. It dug into his dick.

"There are people on the outside who think you're a menace and you shouldn't be alive," Fred said, his voice growly.

Shaq let the plate drop from his hand to settle on the bottom of the sink. Food remnants bobbed around, some rising to the surface. "The same goes for you."

"Yep, but so far, there hasn't been a hit put out on me."

Too late, Shaq realised it wasn't Zebedee he had to worry about. But was he in on this? Had he handed Fred a weapon when the old man had bumped into him? He must have, because whatever dug into Shaq's side didn't feel like a fist. Fists weren't sharp.

"W-what?" Shaq said, his hands surrounded by bits of food and greasy scum.

"I'm afraid this is the end for you."

The sharpness disappeared with Fred's arm flying out to the right, then swooping back to Shaq's side. A punch landed. Shaq had heard being stabbed could be mistaken for a punch, and he waited for the pain. It didn't come, maybe the adrenaline flooding through him saw to that, and as he registered that he was going to die, a sense of being cocooned in the stillness of stalled time took over him. If he wanted to move, he couldn't, he was suspended in a state of disbelief, his flight or fight abandoning him when he needed it the most.

"Say sorry," Fred growled.

"Sorry! Please, don't do this…"

Fred smacked a palm to the back of Shaq's head, forcing it towards the water. Shaq tried to push back against it, but the hold was too strong. Even though he was old, Fred did weights, and all that time working out gave him the advantage.

Shaq's face loomed ever closer to the specks of floating food, and then his brain caught up to the danger and time got a move on. He pushed back again, but his head submerged beneath the surface, the pressure of Fred's hand keeping it there. Shaq stared at his underwater prison, dancing food debris the last thing he was going to see. He thought of his mum, how she'd be gutted he'd been killed.

Fred wrenched Shaq's head up and threw him to the floor. Shaq landed on his side, his hip barking with agony, and he scrabbled to get away from the old man who held a stubby kitchen knife. Blood from the stab wound mixed with water droplets, creating smears on the tiles where Shaq's movement had scuffed it. Fred advanced, getting down on his knees and raising the blade. He brought it down, slicing into Shaq's stomach. Shaq felt that one, and he cried out, lifting a hand to prevent Fred doing it again. The blade sliced his palm, and Shaq glanced at the exit, desperate to make it there, to find help.

Zebedee was back. He blocked the way, thick arms folded.

In a frenzy, Fred stabbed and stabbed. Shaq closed his eyes, accepting the inevitable—what other choice did he have? The agony wouldn't last for long, so if he could just get through this until death claimed him, it'd be all right.

Dayton's face loomed in his mind's eye, and Shaq now believed in karma. He was dying in the same way, and he called out the same thing: "Mum!"

"She won't fucking help you," Fred snarled, issuing punch after punch with the knife. Then he stopped, breathing heavily, and sat on the stomach wounds.

Shaq stared up at him through glassy vision.

Fred looked into Shaq's eyes. "Anaisha says hello. And goodbye…"

That's why he wanted me to say sorry…

The swipe of the knife across Shaq's throat was a blessing.

Zeb didn't care that his part in this would add to his sentence. Like Fred, he was in here with no chance of parole, and to be honest, this excitement was worth being put in segregation. He hadn't had this much fun in a long time.

Fred stood, dropping the knife on the floor. "The urge to do that never dies."

Zeb laughed. "The money doesn't hurt either."

It would arrive in their prison accounts via their family members, enough each week that they'd never go without treats in here, but the main bulk of their payments had been delivered to Zeb's wife and Fred's daughter. Via a phone call Zeb had with his missus earlier, he'd been told what to do, who to rope in to murder Shaq, but not who'd arranged the hit. He didn't care about that either. So long as his wife was well cared for with the readies, that was all that mattered.

An officer doing his walk around the kitchen glanced over at Zeb where he leaned on the wall.

"Fred's had a blip," Zeb said casually. "It's a bit of a mess round here."

Fred laughed, blood splashes all over his face.

The officer came over. Stared at Shaq. "Aww, fucking hell, Frederick!"

Fred smiled at him. "Sorry, pal. Solitary confinement for me, is it?"

Chapter Thirty

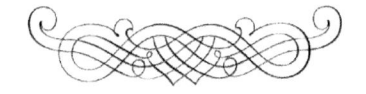

At four o'clock, Anaisha had used a chat box to contact someone at Life Cover Express, her task to get as much information as possible so there was evidence of a scam. She'd left it, at Oliver's urging, that she'd get back to them tomorrow when she'd had a think about whether she could cobble together the five thousand pounds the company had asked for. She'd queried that, asking why she needed to pay such a sum instead of a monthly direct debit of around sixty quid, and they'd assured her it was so she could 'go up a level' in the amount of cover she could have. It sounded like bullshit—it *was* bullshit—and she was determined to help bring them down. It would help take her mind off everything else.

Oliver approached her with someone in a suit she hadn't seen before. A woman. The light-grey fabric gave her a washed-out appearance, and her platinum hairline seemed to merge into her forehead she was that pale.

"Can we borrow you for a minute?" Oliver asked.

Fay stared over, clearly being nosy.

Anaisha blushed at the attention. "Have I done something wrong?"

"Let's go into my office for a chat." Oliver smiled, perhaps trying to allay her fears, then led the way.

Grey Suit trotted after him in her black high heels.

Anaisha followed, her stomach in knots. Had something gone wrong? Had the twins been caught for killing Ben? And what about Shaq? Could it be something to do with him? No, surely Janine would have given her a ring if he was dead.

But maybe she doesn't know yet.

She entered the office and closed the door. Oliver and Grey Suit sat behind his desk, and it felt an awful lot like it must do when facing the firing squad. Her guts churned. At Oliver's gesture, she sat on the chair opposite and tried to calm down.

"This is DCI Theresa Thetford, and she has a few questions for you."

"Okay." Anaisha smiled.

Thetford took a tablet from a briefcase and switched it on, then held in front of her. "You're aware that Benjamin Yeoman took his own life yesterday evening."

"Yes, Janine Sheldon told me."

Thetford glanced up from the tablet and stared directly at Anaisha. "Why did she do it and not Edgar Nelly? After all, he was dealing with your domestic violence claim."

Claim. As if it didn't happen. "She told him she'd do it. We're friends because of what happened to my brother, and she thought it might be best coming from her."

"Ah, Dayton's murder, correct?"

"Yes, Janine led the case. We grew close."

"I see. Where were you on the evening Ben died?"

"At home in my new flat. I had to find somewhere else to live, obviously."

"You did that pretty fast."

Anaisha shrugged. "I got lucky."

"Were you aware Ben owned an unlicensed gun?"

"No. If I was, I'd have reported him for it."

"Did you not come across it when you happened to find the letters Shaq Yarsly sent him?"

"No, like I said, if I had, I'd have reported him."

Where is she going with this? Is she going to accuse me of killing him?

Thetford sniffed. "Would you have any objection to me taking your work and personal phones?"

"No, why would I?"

"Good, good. I'd like to rule you out of any wrongdoing, and your phone records will come in handy for that."

Anaisha frowned and hoped she looked suitably confused. "What kind of wrongdoing? You're not talking about Ben, surely."

"No." Thetford took a few breaths. "Shaq Yarsly was murdered today."

"What? Does Janine know?"

"I don't see why she'd need to be informed. She closed that case a long time ago, as you know. Now, my job is to investigate crimes in prison, hence why I'm here. It's come to my attention that you've visited Mr Yarsly once a month ever since he was placed in custody. Why would you do that?"

"For answers. An apology. And I was trying to show him that people who aren't pure—that's his word, not mine—aren't any different to anyone else."

"I'm aware of his case, I read up on it this afternoon. I understand he killed Dayton because he had a white mother and a black father, correct?"

"So he said."

"What were those visits like?"

"They were okay. I bought him coffee and cakes, asked him why he'd done it. I got the same answer every time."

"So why keep going back?"

"I don't know. I just…I just wanted him to say sorry so I could tell my mum and dad and they could move on. They're stuck. Their life is on hold. They want to make some kind of sense out of what he did."

"I see. And was there any animosity from him during those visits?"

"No. He was calm, never got angry or anything." *He's smug and smarmy and I hate him.*

"Did you?" Thetford paused. "Get angry?"

"No, but I was frustrated. Sad."

"That doesn't gel with what I've seen. After viewing the internal CCTV at the prison, I can tell you that on your most recent visit you bought two cups of coffee, two slices of cake, croissants, and cupcakes. You chatted for a while and at one point seemed angry with him. Why was that?"

"He said something about things being unfair, and I told him what was *unfair* was him taking Dayton away from us. He wound me up, and I retaliated—I shouldn't have given him the satisfaction, to be honest."

"So you just lied to me. About not getting angry."

Anaisha ignored her. "I've already told you I was frustrated. What you saw was exactly that. He apologised. He didn't say sorry outright, but he did give me more of a reason why he killed my brother. I kind of understand now and actually feel sorry for him." *Liar*.

"What reason did he give?"

Anaisha explained about Shaq's teacher. "So he'd had his mind twisted, maybe from an impressionable age, and he must have become so arsey at Dayton for being able to be happy in his own skin that it tipped him over the edge. He had mental health issues, clearly, and if he'd have received help, he may not have committed murder."

"Did he ever mention people called Zebedee Kaatachi and Frederick Engle?"

"No."

"So he didn't give any indication that other inmates had a problem with him?"

"No."

"Mr Kaatachi phoned his wife this morning, as he does every day. She could have passed on a message for him to get Mr Engle to kill Shaq. I'll be speaking to her presently."

"What, and you think I phoned the wife and asked her to do that?"

"No, I'm merely here to gather facts. I don't believe you had anything to do with it. Your record is exemplary, and it's just unfortunate that you visited Mr Yarsly that day—I have to follow that up, you must understand that. I had to ask you those questions so I can eliminate you."

Anaisha wanted to scream. The way Thetford had come across, she'd acted as if Anaisha was a suspect, for God's sake—or was that Anaisha being paranoid? All right, she understood the reasoning—she *could* have approached the wife, but she fucking didn't, the twins must have—but was there any need to be so superior while interviewing her?

Anaisha took her phones out of her pocket and placed them on the desk. "There's nothing on those that's dodgy. When will I get them back?"

"I'll pop them by in about an hour. Digi will download all the data; there's no need for them to keep the phones for an extended period of time. Thank you for speaking with me, and I hope Mr Yarsly's death will give you and your parents some closure." Thetford smiled at Oliver. "Cheers for letting me borrow her. I'll see myself out."

She rose and left the room, clicking the door shut behind her.

"Are you okay?" Oliver asked.

"What the fuck was that all about? She acted like she thought I'd arranged a hit, for fuck's sake."

"I won't tell you to calm down because I value my balls and don't fancy you kneeing me in them, but I have to agree, she was out of line there. Look, why don't you leave early?"

"No, she's coming back with my phones, and anyway—"

"Go and speak to your parents. Tell them the news—about Ben *and* Shaq—then come back for your mobiles."

"Will she be going to see my mum and dad? Will she accuse them of arranging Shaq's murder?"

"She'll likely speak to them, yes, but at least if you warn them she's coming, they won't get a shock like you did. I wish I could have warned *you*, but she insisted on coming with me when I came over to tell you someone was here to question you."

Anaisha sighed. "It's okay, not your fault."

"How do you feel about the news?"

"Relieved he's gone."

"I bet. And Ben?"

"I haven't processed that yet. He basically killed himself so he didn't have to face what he did to me." She absently ran a hand over her bruised cheek. "Coward."

Anaisha had given Mum and Dad the news about Shaq, and they'd rejoiced together. Awful, really, to be pleased someone was dead, but Shaq didn't deserve any pity. But how lovely to see pure joy on their faces at last. When she'd told them about Ben, to explain the state of her face, Dad had gone quiet, then he'd cuddled her and said sorry that he hadn't been there to protect her, like he hadn't been there for Dayton.

"There was nothing you could have done in either case," she'd said.

"I know, but I'm supposed to watch out for my kids, and I didn't."

It had been so weird to laugh and cry at the same time—and *finally*, they'd talked about the funny things Dayton had done and smiled about it instead of bawling. It was the start of healing.

She'd gone back to collect her phones and had to wait an extra hour, emotionally exhausted by the time she'd gone home.

Now, she sat in her flat in the dark in her pyjamas, staring into the middle distance and hoping Shaq burned in Hell. Yes, she felt sorry for the kid he'd been, but only a little. He'd had choices when he'd grown up, he didn't *have* to murder her brother. He'd ripped a Dayton-sized hole in their lives that could never be filled.

A gentle set of taps on the front door alarmed her. She reached for her personal phone in case she needed to use it. She left the light off and wandered down the dark hallway, jumping and screeching when the letterbox flap flipped up.

"It's The Brothers," a man said. "I can see you there, you know."

Shit.

She unlatched the chain and drew the bolts across, then opened the door. With their thick beards and long hair, it took her a moment to gather they were in disguise. She let them in and went back to the living room, putting the light on. She squinted at the glare and turned to find them standing just inside the doorway.

"Thank you," she said. "For what you did. Ben, Shaq, this flat."

"Not a problem. We found out that the teacher was Shaq's uncle. Shaq's cellmate got the information from some notes he'd hidden in their cell. Our PI looked into it. The uncle's dead, got shot in the head, so that's the hat trick done. Someone else likely had a beef with him, too."

Shaq? Did he get his uncle killed? "Thanks. Again."

"How are you fixed for money? I'm George, by the way."

"I do okay."

"It'd be lovely if you didn't have to pay rent, though, wouldn't it, *and* if you had the spare cash to go on holidays abroad and buy nice clothes. Not that what you've got on isn't nice. I quite like pyjamas with cats all over them."

She laughed, although it was a bit unsteady. "What are you getting at?"

"You know Janine's ours, don't you."

"I gathered that."

"And Flint."

"Janine didn't say it in so many words, but yes."

"Flint was the geezer at the Odeon, the one who brought Kendall to us."

"I thought so."

"How about you join him and Janine?"

"I work in the Internet Crime department. I'm not going to be of much use to you."

"It's always good to have people on hand, and we don't exactly need you to do anything at the station, not like Janine and Flint do anyway. We've got something else up our sleeve for you."

She had a feeling she couldn't say no. They had her over a barrel, could get her right in the shit with a few words spoken in the wrong ears. "It's not like I have a choice, is it?"

"No."

"Then I accept."

George smiled. "Good girl. You know it makes sense." He handed her a phone. "Use that to contact us."

She took it. "What do you need me to do?"

"Nothing too taxing. Just keep an eye on Flint. Get friendly with him. Report back to us with anything he says that seems…off."

Off? Don't they trust him? "Is that all?"

Greg nodded.

George grinned. "For now."

She had to ask. "What did Shaq say before he died?"

"Sorry."

"But did he know what he was saying for? Why he was being killed? And who'd arranged it?"

"He did."

All those years of her wishing for that one word, and it had finally happened.

Anaisha sat on the sofa and cried.

Chapter Thirty-One

Mrs Nora Robbins stared at the rubies in her palm. Diamonds studded the outsides of a pendant and matching earrings. Such lovely pieces, ones she wished she could have worn instead of keeping them hidden away. They were the only items that *he* had said were stolen, as per her instructions. The rest had been sold at the pawnshop.

It'd been a heady night when she'd chosen them as part of her stash from the robbery. They signified a time in her life when she'd been desperate, angry, and those gems, amongst others, had saved her skin. She'd been young, and now she was old.

Where had the years gone? How had they flown by so quickly?

She'd just had her hair done at Curls and Tongs, a weekly occurrence. She didn't need the generous discount George had ensured she got, but she'd take it, regardless of whether people thought it was because she was a pensioner. She'd lived frugally as far as outsiders were concerned, yet she'd had more than enough to see her through many years.

Two of her three friends who'd been in on the robbery had died apart from Lucia, who was now a cook at Dolly's Haven. The twins were certainly snapping up the properties in the East End. Not so long ago, she'd seen them outside Curls and Tongs, and her stomach had flipped over. She'd shit herself, thinking they'd found out what she'd done and had come for her. Because the person they'd stolen from was still out there, that infernal bloody man, and in his old age, he might have taken it upon himself to grass Nora and her friends up.

She'd lived in fear of that every day. Wouldn't put it past him at all.

She'd felt bad about that, the murders, but told herself that if the wife had just minded her own business, doing as she'd been told, she wouldn't be dead—and neither would her children. She'd been told to go and stand against the wall with her sons, but she hadn't listened.

The gun against her husband's temple would have spurred her into action, trying to save him.

She'd failed, obviously.

Nora had seen the twins again today. They'd nipped into the salon to see Stacey, the woman who ran it. Nora had tried to earwig on their conversation, but they'd spoken too low, and with all those hairdryers blasting out, it had be nigh on impossible to pick anything up. Their expressions weren't ominous, she'd clocked those in the mirror, so Nora had put it down to The Brothers talking business.

She didn't like them having a reason to be on her housing estate regularly. She'd kept under the radar, hadn't had to struggle to keep her secret from showing itself on her wrinkled face all that often where they were concerned. Maybe she should find another hairdresser. She wouldn't risk bumping into them then.

No, a cheap haircut was a cheap haircut, and she wouldn't turn that down.

What if I ask Stacey to come round mine and do my hair? I can make out I'm having trouble walking.

She chuckled at that. Her legs were just fine, thank you very much, she didn't really need a cane, but a little lie didn't hurt anyone.

Much.

Ask *him* that, and he'd tell you different.

The letterbox clattered, so she placed the rubies in their black velvet bed inside a box and went to the safe behind a painting above the fireplace on her living room wall. Her precious jewels secure, she popped into the hallway to collect the late post. Two bills, a flyer, and a postcard.

She studied the front. Clacton-on-Sea, the image of the sandy beach and the pier stretching out over the water. Maybe her neighbour, Len, had gone there again, but it was odd for him to send her a card. He didn't usually, just bought her a box of fudge as a present for her putting his bins out while he was away. She turned the card over. No writing, but something had been typed. Ah, it must be one of those sales gimmicks, a hotel drumming up business. But how had they got her name? What about data protection?

"Fat lot of good that does."

She read the words.

ENOUGH IS ENOUGH. I CAN'T LIVE LIKE THIS ANYMORE. THERE'S NO ONE LEFT I NEED TO KEEP THE SECRET FROM, SO I MAY AS WELL GO TO THE POLICE. IF YOU DON'T MAKE CONTACT BY THE END OF APRIL, I'LL TAKE IT YOU'RE PREPARED TO SERVE TIME FOR WHAT YOU DID.

The blood drained from Nora's face. It was that fucker, *him*. Had he sent the same card to Lucia? She lived at the refuge, and…

"Fucking hell, someone at Haven might see what it says before she does."

Nora rushed back into the living room, tossing the post on the table beside her recliner. She snatched up her mobile and prodded the screen, selecting Lucia's number.

It rang four rimes.

"All right, Nora?"

"No, I'm not all right, and neither should you be. Has the post arrived there yet?"

"Not that I know of."

"Go and check, for fuck's sake. See if there's a postcard addressed to you."

"A postcard?"

"Just do it, will you? Hurry up!"

Lucia's breathing transferred down the line, then a huff where she must have bent over. The shuffle of paper against paper, a pause, then, "Oh God. Oh no…"

"Exactly. We need to finish this. Kill him like we should have done years ago."

"But we're not spring chickens anymore. Jesus, what about my hip?"

"Take some painkillers. Come round mine, tonight after work. The sooner we make plans the better."

"Right. Right. How did he know where I live now?"

"He must have been keeping tabs on us. Wouldn't you if you were in his position?"

"I suppose so. Look, I'd better go. I left mushrooms cooking in the frying pan."

"Leave after you've made the dinner. You can have some round mine. I'll get a Chinese in and a bottle of wine."

"Okay. See you later."

Nora ended the call and sank onto her chair. She hadn't envisaged murdering anyone at her age, yet here she was.

But it was okay. There was life in the old dog yet.

To be continued in *Rubies*,
The Cardigan Estate 31

Printed in Great Britain
by Amazon